# Wisdom Tree

## Mary Manners

**Wisdom Tree**

Cover Art by *Nicola Martinez*

White Rose Publishing, a division of Pelican Ventures, LLC
www.pelicanbookgroup.com PO Box 1738 *Aztec, NM * 87410

White Rose Publishing Circle and Rosebud logo is a trademark of Pelican Ventures, LLC

Publishing History
Library of Congress Control Number: 2012933361
First White Rose Edition, 2012
Print Edition ISBN 978-1-61116-166-3
Electronic Edition ISBN 978-1-61116-165-6
**Published in the United States of America**

## Dedication

To all the dedicated teachers at Elmwood School in Elmwood Park, IL who took precious time to encourage my writing when I was a student there long ago, especially Miss Moreale, Miss Vestuto, and Miss Carr, I remember you fondly and will be forever grateful to each of you. May God bless you all.

# Praise for Mary Manners

**Contests:**

*Mended Heart* nominated Best Inspirational Romance 2010 by the Romance Reviews

*Tender Mercies* Finalist, 2011 Inspirational Readers Choice Awards, 2nd Place in The Lories Best Published Contest

**Reviews/Comments:**

Tender Mercies, 4 1/2 Stars by The Romantic Times, "...a wonderful read..."

Mended Heart, 4 Stars by The Romantic Times, "...the emotions and secrets revealed make for a poignant story of change..."

Light the Fire, 4 Stars by The Romantic Times, "Manners does an incredible job of putting together a story that not only teaches a valuable lesson, but allows readers to see that a life without mistakes is an impossible dream."

## Other titles by Mary Manners

Mended Heart
Tender Mercies
Light the Fire
Buried Treasures

**Micro-stories**
Brenna's Choice
Starfire

**Sweet Treats Bakery Series**
Kate's Kisses
Grace's Gold
Tessa's Teacakes
Mattie's Meltaways

**Lone Creek Ranch Series**
Lost in Lone Creek
Lullaby in Lone Creek
Lesson in Lone Creek
Love in Lone Creek

**Miracles at Mills Landing
(Coming Soon)**
Miracles and Mischief
Stolen Miracles
Miracles and Dreams

*Teach us to number our days aright,*
*that we may gain a heart of wisdom.*
*~Psalm 90:12~*

# 1

She'd tried to kill him.

Jake swallowed an oath and cut the motor on the mower he wrestled through overgrown September grass. His heart thundered like a runaway semi as his gaze locked on the woman's startling green eyes, framed by a wisp of sun-kissed blonde hair. She was shorter than he was—quite a bit shorter—and willowy as a ribbon in the wind, but the strappy sandals hugging her feet added a bit of height.

"Have you lost your mind?" The words tumbled out before Jake could get a hold on them. "I might have run over you, hacked off a few of your toes." He quickly regretted his harsh tone when her smile wilted. Her gaze lowered to her feet, and she wiggled her pink-polished toes.

"But you didn't, and I'm still in one piece. So..." She had a slight Southern accent, a soft lilting voice that he imagined could flash to a bite in an instant.

Jake drew a long, calming breath laced with the sweet scent of freshly mown grass as he swiped a forearm across his brow. Sweat trickled down his back, making his T-shirt cling to damp skin. "Don't you know you're not supposed to sneak up on people when they're working with dangerous equipment?"

"Of course." Her gaze narrowed as she crossed her arms and lifted her chin. He imagined her lack of height was no deterrent to getting her way, and her tone might have scalded the first few layers of skin from him. "But I didn't sneak up on you."

"Could have fooled me." He huffed out a breath and wished he wasn't feeling so short-tempered. It gave the wrong impression, especially here at church, and with someone new. He tugged the collar of his T-shirt and hoped for a cool breeze, trying not to think about how he was in a hurry to pick up Corey, and that he didn't have time for chit-chat. But he'd make time…he always did. It was part of his job. "I sure didn't hear you coming."

"I called to you, but you're *mowing*." She enunciated the word as if she thought he might be a few cards short of a Pinochle deck. "That's most likely why you didn't hear me."

"Yeah, that's just my point." Jake's restraint was sorely tested by the smug gleam in her eye. His gaze grazed her crisp linen jacket over a flowered sundress that caressed a lithe figure. She looked graceful and cool under the blistering glare of the sun.

Jake, on the other hand, was sweltering to the point of self-combustion. He hadn't intended to mow the grass, but when Bill Rogers, the church caretaker, called in with a sick daughter, there wasn't time to find help. So Jake stepped in to pick up the slack. He brushed prickly blades of mulched grass from his faded jeans and gestured toward the mower. "Care to give it a go?"

She took a giant step back. "No thanks. I'm not…properly dressed." She surveyed him, shielding her eyes from the sun that burned from a cloudless blue sky. Her other hand disappeared into the tote slung over one shoulder. "Drink?" She offered him a bottle of water. "You look like you can use some cooling off."

Jake reached for the water. His pulse rate was beginning to ease, and thirst won out over pride. "Thanks."

"You're welcome."

She gaped as he uncapped the bottle and guzzled the cool water in little more than a gulp then swiped stray droplets from his mouth with the back of his hand.

"Do you need to sit down for a minute? You look...winded."

"No. I'm almost done." Jake wouldn't have chosen jeans that morning if he'd known he was going to have to mow; cargo shorts would have been a better choice. The thick denim held heat against his skin like a sauna. "Ahh, that's good. Do you make it a habit to carry bottled water with you?"

"Nope...it's your lucky day." She adjusted the tote over her shoulder, and he saw it was filled with papers bundled neatly together by an array of colorful, plastic-coated clips. "Who knew I'd stumble across a hot groundskeeper in need."

Jake did a double-take when her smile turned down and her gaze flashed complete mortification at the unintended double meaning. He tugged his ball cap low over his eyes and crossed his arms as she stuttered through an explanation.

"I-I mean, you're hot from mowing..." she gulped, shading her eyes from his gaze. "Because it's so hot out here, and you need—"

"Wow." Jake burst into laughter. He fought hard to regain his composure as tears stung his eyes and mixed with the sweat on his brow to blur his vision.

"Hey." Her cheeks flushed and blonde curls bobbed haughtily as she crossed her arms, threw her shoulders back, and gave him a seething look. "Don't you know it's not nice to laugh at someone else's expense?"

Jake coughed into a hand and dipped his head to hide his grin. "Sorry, but you stepped right into that one."

A crimson splotch crept up her neck and crawled across her face. "OK, I guess I did. Anyway—"

"I'm Jake." He wiped his hand on his jeans in an attempt to brush off some of the sweat and dirt before extending it to her.

"Carin." She grasped his hand and gave it a tentative shake. The scent of sandalwood perfume clung to the humid air, and Jake inhaled deeply, his pulse easing down another notch.

"So, what brings you here today, Carin?"

She tucked a stray curl behind one ear and trained those pretty green eyes on him. "I need to speak with the pastor of this church. I was hoping you could help me locate him."

"Maybe I can." Jake leaned lazily against the mower. She was neat and tidy, all business, while he stood sweaty and covered head to toe in mulched grass that had been swept up on a breeze. Maybe it was the heat, or her smug expression, or perhaps the fact he was in a bit of a foul mood and only human, after all, but he decided to have a little fun. "Which pastor are you looking for—youth or senior?"

"I…um…I don't know." She caught her lower lip between her teeth, gnawed for a moment and then let go. "I didn't think to ask. I suppose he must be the youth pastor. Senior pastors tend to be older, I assume."

Jake stifled a groan. She'd conveyed the typical sentiment. By all accounts, he should be a balding, stooped over, crotchety old man. The thought raised his ire even more. "Well, the youth pastor stepped out for a while. Meetings and planning sessions…you know how pressing church matters can be. Was he expecting you?"

"No, but…I was hoping to speak with him, confidentially."

The disappointment in her gaze caused Jake a slight prick of guilt. His voice softened, and he remembered why he was here at the church in the first place. "Is what you need to speak about an emergency of some sort?"

"No!" Carin emphasized the word. "I mean, no, I wouldn't want to worry him. It's not pressing. I just need to…" The words died in her throat.

"Are you sure it's not an emergency?" He couldn't leave her hanging if it truly was a pressing issue.

"Sure, I'm sure."

Jake debated. It wasn't an emergency, and she'd be back in a day or so if he played his cards right. Then he wouldn't be in a hurry to get Corey, and he'd have all the time in the world to talk with her—a better prospect, all the way around.

"Tell you what," Jake coaxed. "Why don't you come back

Sunday morning for the ten o'clock service, when both pastors are sure to be here, and I can personally guarantee that following the service whichever pastor you need to speak with will give you his undivided attention for as long as you'd like."

"You're positive?" One eyebrow rose into a smooth little arch. "What I need to speak about could take a while."

He nodded.

She jostled the bag on her shoulder and sighed, her gaze scanning the steps that led into the church. "Well...that's just the day after tomorrow. I suppose it can wait until then. Ten o'clock, you said?"

"For the service, yes. And you can do your talking afterwards."

"I don't want to divulge the details." Her forehead creased as her eyebrows knit together. "But perhaps I should leave a short message in the office, maybe a note with the secretary."

"No need." Jake tried not to glance at his watch. Corey would be waiting at the ball field, and who knew what kind of mischief he'd get into if Jake was delayed too long. "Besides, the secretary's gone home for the day. But you have my word; the pastor will be OK with you showing up."

"You're sure?"

Jake eyed her...abundant ringlets of soft blonde curls, tidy appearance, and eyes that said she didn't think he could possibly know anything about the pastor. The slight prick of guilt he'd felt fled. "I'm sure."

"Well..." Carin wound a strand of curl around an index finger. "Thank you...I guess."

"No problem." The late-afternoon sun silhouetted her figure. She had to be a runner—or perhaps a dancer. Though her figure was slight, Jake noticed the definition of supple calf muscles below the hem of her skirt. He drew his gaze away. "I'd better get back to work now...unless you'd care to stay and help."

She pressed a finger to the forehead crease and gnawed

her lower lip again while readjusting the tote. "No. I've…um…got errands to run."

*Yeah, right,* Jake thought as she backed away. *You wouldn't want to dirty those freshly-manicured nails.*

"Well, the invitation's open…anytime." He swept a hand across the clipping-littered sidewalk. "There's always plenty of lawn to mow."

"I'll…um…remember that."

The mortified look on her face was priceless, and Jake grinned as she hastily retreated to her car. "Thanks for your help."

"See you Sunday?" Jake called.

"Of course…if you're here."

"Oh, I'll be here."

"Me, too." The way she said it, her voice lilting with a biting edge to it, made Jake wonder exactly what was up. Now he had no choice but to wait to find out. Guess that was the price he'd pay for letting the heat—and a bit of temper—get the best of him.

He thought about going after her, but the compact sedan's engine rumbled to life before he had time to make up his mind. As the car puttered from the lot, Jake checked his watch and quickly turned his attention back to mowing. He crushed the empty water bottle and stuffed it into the back pocket of his jeans before double-timing it through the last section of lawn. Then he wrestled the mower back into the shed, brushed off his jeans, and went inside the church long enough to wash grass from his hands and check his voicemail. The last bit of mowing gave him time to reflect, and guilt gnawed at him.

He wondered what Carin wanted. He shouldn't have run her off without asking. What kind of pastor was he, anyway? What if it was important? What if she didn't come back?

৵৵

*Who on earth does he think he is? The arrogant, filthy, grass-covered bohemian. Why, I'll—*

The shriek of a horn startled Carin, and she slammed the brakes, skidding toward oncoming traffic. "Oh!" She held her breath as tires squealed over pavement and her car came to rest mere inches from the pickup truck in front of her. The odor of burning rubber coupled with fear made her gag. "Sorry," she gasped, as if the driver of the truck might hear.

Oh, why on earth had she allowed Hailey to talk her into moving from her job helping her dad at his law firm in Nashville to take a teaching job at East Ridge Middle...and seventh grade, to boot? Middle school kids were a far cry from the affluent adults who came into her dad's upscale firm to seek his advice on everything from basic living wills to complicated estate planning and civil suits. But she had a degree in English, and East Ridge Middle needed a qualified English teacher when Mrs. Baldwin, a thirty-five year veteran, decided to retire. So when Hailey called and suggested the move, Carin had jumped at the chance to take over. She'd always loved the Tennessee Valley and the foothills of the Smoky Mountains, and there wasn't much anymore to keep her in Nashville.

Except for her dad, and he was pretty much busy at his law firm all the time.

Besides, she needed a change to get away from the memories...the grief of losing her mom and then Cameron, and of the turmoil that had followed with Phillip, too. Nothing else she tried seemed to work. A change of scenery—a bit of distance—was the answer for her troubled heart.

But it wasn't easy being the new kid on the block at East Ridge Middle, especially when she demanded the absolute best from her students. During the first few weeks, chaos nearly choked her, but she finally had a handle on things—a routine and a plan she was more than satisfied with.

Except for Corey Samuels. Apparently he reigned as King of Chaos.

The kid had a chip on his shoulder the size of Montana, with an attitude to match. To say his grades and effort were underwhelming put it mildly. But his records showed top test scores and well-above-average ability, and something in his eyes told her there was more to the story. He reminded her of her younger brother, Cameron. As she tamped the urge to throttle Corey when he blew spit wads at her white board and made rude comments under his breath, something about him tugged at her heartstrings.

No one had been able to help Cameron, and the end result was nothing less than heartbreaking. She missed her brother, gone nearly a year now. The pain of his death never left her.

When she asked Hailey for guidance concerning Corey, her friend mentioned that a talk with Corey's brother might help. So on the way home she'd swung by the church where Hailey said he was a pastor, but confidentiality had kept her from searching for him past that behemoth caretaker.

Carin expelled a long breath and released her hands from their death grip on the steering wheel. She wouldn't allow that poor excuse of a caretaker get to her, even if he *did* almost run her over with the hulking, dilapidated piece of junk-metal he called a mower.

A second horn blared, and Carin sprang to attention as traffic began to flow southbound toward the outskirts of town.

*Just wait until Sunday, Mr. Lawnmower Man. I'm tougher than I look. I'll show you…*

# 2

Jake pulled into the ball field to find Corey gathering his football equipment and stuffing it into an oversized duffle bag. The sun was a sinking bronze glow in the late-afternoon sky, and most of the other middle-school players were gone, but Jake knew Corey always hung around longer to get in all the practice he possibly could. He'd live at the ball field if Jake would allow it. And some days Jake considered this, just for the chance to restore short snippets of quiet to his life.

"Hey, how'd it go?" Jake called as he slid out of the Jeep and loped over to toss a scuffed football into the battered bag.

"Pretty good." Corey swung around to face him. His forehead was smudged with dirt, his cheeks painted with eye-black that he insisted blocked out the glare of the sun. The scents of damp earth and grass clung to his uniform. "Coach McCrosky asked me to demonstrate some plays today. He says my throw is really improving."

"Well, that's certainly good news. The extra practice is paying off, huh?"

"Yeah." Corey nodded, and shaggy black hair hid his cobalt-blue eyes. He had their mom's eyes, wide and sensitive, while Jake looked more like their father. "He says with a little more practice, I'll have the whole package."

"The whole package, huh?" Jake grinned and ruffled Corey's matted hair. At the rate Corey was growing, Jake wouldn't be able to do that much longer. He could hardly keep the kid in jeans…and forget about tennis shoes. They'd set up a frequent buyer account at the Nike outlet and were on a first-name basis with the owner. "Coach McCrosky wouldn't, by any chance, be alluding to both excellent grades and outstanding athletic abilities as part of this whole package, would he?"

"Please don't start on my grades." Corey groaned as he zipped the duffle bag and swung it over his shoulder, then reached for his helmet. "I still have a headache from last night's lecture."

"But I'm your big brother. I'm supposed to hassle you about your grades."

"I know. Like you'd ever let me forget."

"I'd be dropping the ball if I did." Jake smacked him on the back. "Couldn't do that now, could I?"

"Sometimes you're a real pain in the neck, you know."

"Uh-huh." Jake twirled his key ring on an index finger and the metal jangled. "It's a big brother's job to be a pain in the neck."

"Then you must be the CEO of big brothers, big brother."

"You've got that right." Jake made an effort to keep things light as they headed toward the Jeep. He was in no mood for a battle tonight. Corey had been living with him nearly eight months, and although Jake hated to admit it, he was more than a little concerned about Corey's effort and attitude at school. Their parents' unexpected death had ripped a gaping hole in the routine of their lives, and for Corey that meant moving away from everything that was familiar, to a new school…new friends. If it weren't for his love of football, there was no telling what trouble he'd be getting himself into. But if his grades didn't come up and his attitude didn't improve— soon—football might not even remain an option much longer.

"I'm starving. I could eat two horses." Corey loped toward the Jeep. "Can we stop at Pete's Burger Palace? *Please?*"

"Again?" Jake grimaced. "I don't know if my stomach can survive it. Aren't you tired of greasy little hamburgers?"

"Uh-uh. Where else can you get all the important food groups in half-a-dozen easy-to-gulp sliders?"

"I keep telling you ketchup in not a vegetable."

"Is, too." Corey tossed his bag into the backseat of the

Jeep and climbed up front to settle in beside Jake.

"The next thing you'll tell me is that chocolate's a dairy product because it's made with milk."

Corey buckled his seat belt and reached for the radio dial. "Works for me."

Jake sighed and cranked the ignition. Music filled the cab, and the floor of the Jeep vibrated beneath his feet. "OK, I'll let you gorge on burgers, but then it's straight home to start your homework." He reached for the volume, turned the heavy base down to a more palatable tone.

"But it's Friday night." Corey's gaze widened with mortification. He reached for the volume dial but retreated when Jake waved him off. "Dillon wants to hang out."

"Great. He can hang out at our place." Jake shifted into first gear, then second, and headed toward the road. "Tell him to bring his schoolbooks. You can study together."

"No way." The eye roll was perfected from hours of practice. "I was thinking we could go to the arcade."

"No." Jake shook his head. "I know what goes on there, Corey, and you're not going to be a part of it."

"But *everyone* goes there."

"Not *everyone*. Because *you* aren't. And I don't think Patrick and Julie would allow Dillon to go either. At least not on a Friday night when it's swarming with high school and college kids, getting into who-knows-what."

"You sound just like Dad."

Jake's heart tore, but he kept a steady face. "I'll take that as a compliment."

"I miss him and Mom."

"I know you do." Jake trained his gaze on the road but reached over to give Corey's knee a quick squeeze. "I do, too."

"Anyway," Corey continued, sighing with tortured exaggeration. "I've been praying for you."

"You have?" Jake was cautious. Since the accident, Corey had been anything but open to prayer. He was angry, and most often that anger was directed at God—with Jake a close second.

"Sure. I've been praying for God to send you a girlfriend, so maybe you'll go out on Friday nights like a normal adult. Then I could spend time with my friends and have a life."

"Corey, that's not...funny," Jake sputtered. A woman in his life was the last thing on his mind. His plate was full—overflowing—with church and keeping Corey out of trouble. And since Corey had become a huge part of his life—a very demanding part—peace and quiet had flown right out the window. But at least Corey had mentioned prayer. It was a step in the right direction. "So you think I'm normal, huh?"

"Well, it *is* a stretch of the imagination."

"Gee, thanks."

"No problem."

"Maybe you should pray for something else, like some improvement in your grades. Because if I dated on Friday nights, I'd have to find someone to babysit you so you wouldn't try to sneak out to the arcade or the mall and get into all kinds of trouble."

Corey's jaw dropped and his eyes flew wide. "*Babysit me?*" He gagged on the words. "Oh, brother. I don't need a babysitter. I'm almost thirteen, in case you haven't noticed."

"Oh, believe me...I've noticed." Now Jake rolled his eyes.

"Yeah, right." Corey slid down in his seat and crossed his arms, working up a good sulk. Dirt clung to his fingernails. "But you still treat me like I'm six."

"What homework do you have?" Jake asked. Might as well dig all the way in and make the adolescent sulk worth putting up with. "We'll get it done tonight because I have to officiate at the Grayson wedding tomorrow morning, and then run by the hospital for that fundraiser."

"Why do I have to go, too?"

"Because the last time I left you home alone, I got a phone call from Mrs. Jenson. You and Dillon rigged a ramp across the creek and went stunt-jumping on your skateboards, remember?"

"She's such a snoop."

"She was just looking out for you—and your bones."

"I can't have any fun without someone snitching on me."

"Well, don't do anything they'd want to snitch about."

"Bor-ing."

"Maybe, but you'll survive it. Anyway, if you want to go to the ballgame with Dillon after church Sunday, you have to get your homework done tonight. End of story. So, what do you have?"

"Just some English, if you really have to know." Corey huffed and stared out the window as a breeze whipped his hair across his forehead. "And by the way, I despise English. I think I might start speaking a foreign language in protest— anything but English. I wish Mrs. Baldwin didn't retire. Everyone says she was easy and fun, and this new teacher's such a dictator she makes even *you* look like a real softie."

"Impossible." Jake tapped the brake as they came to a red light. "But I can toughen up even more if you'd like."

"No, thanks." Corey shook his head. "This teacher's more ruthless than King Henry the Eighth. We're learning about him in social studies."

"You don't say. And the English teacher…?"

"Miss O'Malley." Corey shrugged. "She thinks English is the only class on the face of the earth. She makes us write until our fingers fall off. She's, like, the writing Nazi. Dillon and I are thinking about starting a petition to ban all the writing. I'll bet every kid in the school would sign it. Then she'd have to back off. She must be killing a million trees a day with it. There has to be some Go Green law she's breaking. Besides, I think I'm developing writer's elbow or something." To prove his point, he rubbed his arm through the sleeve of his dirt-splattered football jersey.

"Is that so?" Jake glanced at him. "Maybe a little time away from the football field would cure that problem. Throwing a football can't be good if you hurt that much. And the extra study time might haul your grades from the cellar."

"No!" Corey's eyes widened as he wagged his head. "I mean, we wouldn't really start a petition. Dillon's mom would ground him for life."

"And you think I wouldn't do the same to you?"

"Yeah, yeah, I know." Corey sighed, shoulders slumped. "I guess this is where I'm supposed to say I'll try harder."

"Only if you mean it."

"I do, I guess..." Corey hesitated, and Jake knew instinctively that more was coming. "But...well...Miss O'Malley wants to have a conference with you."

"Is that so?"

"Don't worry. I told her you're on an extended cruise to the Caribbean, and when you return you'll probably be too busy to meet with her. Besides, you're just glad I'm not planning to run away to that commune in Tasmania anymore—"

"You did not! Corey, I'm going to—"

"Gotcha!" Corey grinned as if he'd just told the best joke in the world.

"I am not amused, little brother. You'd better get serious real quick."

At the stern tone of Jake's voice, Corey sobered immediately. "She said she was going to call the church, since Miss Jackson—um, Hailey, told her that's where you work."

*Hailey...she teaches a Sunday school class at the church. How is she connected to all this?*

"But I guess she forgot, so I just snitched on myself. Pretty dumb, huh?"

"Hmmm..." Jake's mind flashed back to mowing...and to jewel-green eyes framed by soft blonde curls that danced on a gentle breeze. "What's Miss O'Malley's first name?"

"I dunno. Carin, I think. But we all call her Slasher because she scribbles notes in neon green pen from one end of our papers to the other. She calls it critiquing, but when we get the papers back they look like alien creatures have puked all over them. Even Amy MacGregor can't snag so much as a *B* from the Slasher, and Amy *always* makes *A's* in *everything*."

Jake drummed the steering wheel with grass-stained fingertips. "What does Miss O'Malley look like?"

Corey shrugged. "She's got curly blonde hair about this

long." He lifted a hand to his shoulder. "And she talks, like, nonstop and she's got these laser-green eyes that just kind of bore right through you when she's lecturing you, which she does *a lot*. And…"

Jake remembered the petite woman with a smug grin and an attitude to match that he'd shared words with earlier that afternoon. In his mind's eye he saw her abundant blonde curls and deep emerald eyes that had seared right through him as he'd laughed at her twist of words. So this was Carin O'Malley, A.K.A. Slasher.

"Hey, you're not listening." Corey jabbed a finger into Jake's shoulder. "What's wrong? You look like you've seen a ghost."

"Not a ghost, little brother, but someone much more intriguing."

"I don't get it."

"Oh, but you will." Jake's cryptic response left Corey blissfully speechless. Sunday might prove to be more explosive than a Fourth-of-July finale.

# 3

A stab of homesickness speared Carin as she slipped a frozen dinner into the microwave at her small rental house. Though she'd lived there nearly four months, she'd had little time to decorate, and the walls were still painfully bare. She'd managed to arrange a few baskets along the cabinet tops and had found a set of floral canisters at the home supply store that she'd filled and set on the counter.

The phone call from Phillip hadn't helped. When his number popped up on her cell phone caller ID, she'd known better than to answer, but he'd caught her off guard—again.

"Let's talk things out, Carin. We can fix this." His voice slid over the line, deep and smooth as warm molasses. She figured that's what had lured her in the first place—the smooth talk.

"There's nothing to discuss."

"Be reasonable." The tone of his voice had escalated when he realized she wasn't going to cave. "Your father's starting to ask questions."

Panic stabbed her. "What are you telling him?"

"What do you want me to tell him?"

*The truth*, she thought, but knew that wasn't the answer. The truth would wound her father, because he'd thought of Phillip like a son since Cameron had died.

"You can't frighten me anymore." The lie scorched her lips. He *did* frighten her. He could hurt her—again—without so much as a second thought. "Quit calling me, Phillip. Just leave me alone."

"Aw, baby, stop this nonsense and come home. I want you back."

"What?" Bile rose in Carin's throat. She gagged. "Are you serious—after what you did? After all the lies? This is my home now. I'm not coming back to Nashville."

She heard him breathing on the other end, weighing his words carefully as the microwave whirred and her fluffy gray cat, Scooter, motored restlessly around her feet.

"Maybe I should come to see you...work this out face to face." The words were laced with threat.

"No!" She'd get a restraining order if she had to, not that it would do any good. A year at the law firm, writing and filing reports, had made that perfectly clear. "If you even try to come near me, I'll...I'll—"

"You're guilty, too." The words scalded. "Just as guilty as I am—maybe even more. You let Cameron down. You weren't there for him...not when he needed you most."

Carin gasped and jabbed the end button, then tossed the phone on the counter as if it had burst into flames, burning her. Phillip's words echoed like thunder in her ears.

*You're guilty, too. Maybe even more.*

He was right to some degree. Even now, the thought tore at Carin.

The microwave chimed. She drew the meal from the turntable and dumped it in the sink. Her stomach soured, and her appetite fled.

How was she ever going to step foot in church tomorrow to follow up on the issue with Corey Samuels? Surely God would take one look at her striding through the door and strike her down, quick as lightning. She had no place there, yet she had to go.

The kid—Corey—needed her. He was in crisis; she felt it in her gut. And she couldn't let him down. Not like she'd let Cameron down. No, sir. Not again—never again.

❧

"She won't show up," Jake muttered as he organized sermon notes at his office desk. He struggled with a serious case of guilt because his mind was as far from the message he was about to share as the sun is from Pluto. Instead, his head was filled with images of curly blonde hair and fiery emerald eyes set in a round, determined face. And that voice…full of frustration with a hint of indignation as Carin O'Malley stood in the warm sunlight with arms crossed, the scents of sandalwood and freshly-mown grass dancing around her.

*No, she'll show up. If Corey's been pulling the same old stunts, she definitely will.* Corey's antics, especially at school, could easily fill a notebook cover to cover.

"Who on earth are you talking to?" Corey loped through the office doorway and glanced around. Seeing no one but Jake, he shook his head. "You're losing it, Jake, talking to yourself."

"Maybe so." Jake forced his mind to focus. It was no wonder he was going crazy. Worrying about Corey, keeping up with his duties at the church, and now Carin O'Malley—A.K.A. Slasher—tossed into the mix, really stirred things up. There was only so much one person could handle, even with God's help. "Take my sermon notes and lay them on the podium near the altar. Keep them in order, OK?"

"Sure. But how can you make heads or tails of any of this?" Corey flipped the papers, which were stained with muddy-brown splotches.

"I did battle with the coffeemaker last night." Jake had done battle with more than the coffeepot. Memories had played havoc with him, and sleep had been a long time coming. He shouldn't have toyed with Carin O'Malley. "But it all makes sense, at least to me, so don't mix up the pages."

"Whatever." A clatter down the hall drew Corey's attention. "Dillon's here. His mom's probably arrived early to get the music ready for the service."

Julie Raulston was East Ridge Church's music director, and a savant as far as anything musical was concerned. She'd taught Dillon to play the guitar and had begun to work with Corey, as well, since he showed some interest in learning.

"Can Dillon and I go out back and toss a baseball until the

service begins?"

"Sure, just remember…no batting in the parking lot. You know what happened last time?"

"How could I forget?"

He'd smashed a beauty of a homerun right through the windshield of Mr. Humphrey's brand-spanking-new extended-cab Ford Ranger.

"You grounded me for a whole week."

"Because you disobeyed me, and you deserved to be grounded." Jake jabbed a finger in Corey's direction. "So stick to throwing and don't be late for the service."

"We won't be." Corey's mouth twisted into a scowl. "Dillon's mom would lecture him for, like, three years. And I don't even want to think about what you would do."

"A little fear is good." Jake switched off the computer on his side-desk, remembering the favorite phrase his dad would share whenever Jake tested the boundaries as a boy. "Just consider the consequences."

"Whatever. Gotta go. Dillon's waiting."

Corey spun in the doorway and bounded down the hall, dark hair flying as his tennis shoes slapped freshly-waxed tile.

"Give me patience, Lord. Make me strong." Jake lifted his eyes to the heavens and prayed.

"Maybe this will help." Patrick Raulston came through the doorway to hand Jake a foam cup filled with coffee. "Fresh from the kitchen. You look like you can use a strong jolt of java."

"Thanks." Jake downed a sip, and the bitter brew warmed his tongue. "Ahh…hits the spot."

"Rough night?" Patrick slipped into a chair near the desk and scratched his short-cropped beard. He had an easy laugh, and his eyes, the color of bright copper pennies, rarely failed to smile. He and Julie made a good team; their interests were similar since Patrick worked at the church as a youth pastor. They'd met years ago, while on a summer-long mission trip to inner-city Philadelphia. Marriage and children had quickly followed.

"Just a little sleepless."

"Corey OK?"

"Maybe...I don't know." Jake scratched his chin, and felt the makings of a five o'clock shadow, though it was barely nine o'clock in the morning. He'd shaved, hadn't he? He struggled to remember...the morning was a blur. "I think one of his teachers is stopping by today...Miss O'Malley?"

"Carin O'Malley?" Patrick leaned forward in the chair and placed his coffee cup on the edge of Jake's desk. "I've heard Hailey Jackson mention her. The two are good friends."

"Ahh, so *there's* the link."

"Excuse me?" Patrick smoothed his beard again.

"Just mumbling to myself. Forget it." Jake downed another gulp of coffee. "Did you get a quote on the materials for the playground renovations?"

Patrick pulled a slip of paper from the pocket of his khakis. "I did, and the estimate came in significantly higher than we planned. So, we'll either have to shelve the project or do the lion's share of the work ourselves."

"Well, shelving it's not an option." Jake took the paper and scanned the figures Patrick had jotted. "We need to consider the safety of the kids. If we don't give the playground area the facelift it desperately needs, someone's bound to get hurt playing out there...eventually. And that's unacceptable."

"I agree." Patrick drained his cup, crushed the foam, and tossed it into the trash can beside Jake's desk. "So, should we move forward with the plan?"

"Let's make an announcement today—a call for volunteers—and see who signs on. I'll bet we get a decent turnout."

"Sounds like a step in the right direction. I'll firm up the details with the trustees and ask Stuart to order the materials. They should arrive by next weekend."

"Good. Now, we'd better head to the sanctuary. I hear the halls coming to life."

"Hold up." Patrick shifted in the chair and lowered his voice. "You know I never mince words and, well, I have to tell you that I sense a restlessness in you, Jake."

"I have been a bit out of sorts." Jake ran a hand through his hair. "This issue with Corey—and school—it's keeping me up at night. I'm failing him, Patrick. He needs more than I can give. I don't know what else to do to help him. I'd hoped with time things would improve, but it's just not getting any better."

"That's where God steps in."

"He doesn't seem to be listening."

"Oh, but He is. No one's more covered in prayer than you...and Corey. Be patient. Give God time to work in His way."

"I'm tired, Patrick." Jake pressed a hand to his eyes, then rubbed the scruff of his chin as a wave of tension swept across his back.

"I know." Patrick's brown eyes were round with concern. He patted Jake's shoulder. "Just hang in there a little longer, OK? Everything will ease into place before too much longer."

"OK." Jake nodded and swallowed hard. Patrick was an anchor, the most devout man he knew. Jake wondered where he'd be without Patrick's friendship and counsel. He'd trust the man of God with his life.

"You can lean on me and Julie. We're here to help."

"And both of you are godsends, for sure." Jake sighed and turned toward the doorway. "I hear Mrs. Doran laughing in the hallway."

The elderly woman had a distinctive laugh—deep and raspy from throat surgery she'd had a few years ago. Going on fifty-three years of marriage, she and Mr. Doran still treasured each other's company. Jake longed for that kind of relationship, prayed for it, but God had yet to bless him with anything even remotely close. The Dorans started hazelnut coffee brewing in the church kitchen, and Mrs. Doran always poured Jake a steaming mug with extra cream. Then the couple set out platters of doughnuts and sweet rolls brought from the bakery they owned. The chocolate pastries covered in a sweet glaze with colorful sprinkles were Jake's favorite. Mrs.

Doran knew this, so she always saved two for him—one for now and one for later, she always said.

"I wonder if she brought my favorite doughnuts today," Jake mused.

"Of course she did." Patrick's low laugh rumbled. "She hasn't missed a Sunday since you've been here, has she?"

"Not that I can recall." Jake shook his head, glancing into the hall.

Mr. Staley arrived next. Eighty-three and widowed for nearly two years, he no longer drove a car but lived in a house down the street and still walked with a spring in his step. Jake could set his watch by Mr. Staley's arrival.

Soon the high school and local college kids arrived. They congregated on wrought-iron benches beneath shady maple trees in the front churchyard to gobble doughnuts and share their adventures from the week.

One by one, people sailed into the sanctuary to settle in their usual places. It had been awfully tough two years ago when Jake became head pastor of the church. A month shy of twenty-eight, he had been younger than many of the members of the congregation and some hadn't exactly welcomed him with open arms. But he'd worked tirelessly to gain their respect. And now they accepted Corey, too, despite his rough edges and reckless bent toward mischief.

"I'm Corey's prayer warrior," Mrs. Doran had shared with Jake last week when she brought him a pastry. "I know his faith's being tested, and he's struggling, Pastor Jake. But don't you worry about a thing…I've got him covered in prayer. The Lord's working on him, just wait and see."

Her gracious words, the gentle but sure tone of her voice, had brought much-needed comfort. *I've been so blessed, despite the mountains in my path. I have to remember that during times like these. God has a perfect plan…*

Jake did a quick inventory of the crowd to see who had arrived for the service—and who hadn't.

Miss Carin O'Malley definitely hadn't…yet.

Corey was seated in the third row along with Dillon and

several other middle school kids. A hush fell over the crowd as Julie began to play a soft melody on the keyboard while Patrick settled in among a group of younger children. Jake meandered toward the front of the sanctuary, shaking a few hands and sharing pleasantries along the way.

Arriving at his seat, Jake glanced over his sermon notes one last time then smoothed his shirt and jacket. As Julie finished the Call to Worship he rose, cleared his throat, and turned to face the congregation for opening prayer.

And paused.

Carin O'Malley slipped into a seat beside Corey, looking pretty in a soft peach sundress and sandals that might be called anything but sensible.

She turned and their gaze met. Jake noted the confusion that registered for a fleeting moment in her emerald eyes before her cheeks reddened in astonishment. Her chin came up and her lips moved as she muttered under her breath. Penned in beside her, Corey fidgeted like a caged panther. If Jake lived to be ninety he'd never forget the shock on Corey's face as he realized the infamous Slasher and his big brother were…hmm… acquainted.

"Good morning. I'm glad to see a few new faces here." Jake gazed directly into Carin's indignant eyes. "Welcome to East Ridge Church. We're glad to have you here with us today. Let us bow our heads and pray."

Jake lowered his gaze and drew a deep, cleansing breath. Prayer was no time for mischief, even in a situation such as this. He cleared his mind of all thought and focused on his Lord and Savior.

"Dear Lord, thank You for this beautiful day and for bringing us together to worship You in all Your glory. May this service bring honor to You, and may You fill us with Your Holy Spirit as we praise and honor Your name. Let us live our lives for You, Lord, and may Your words light each step of our path. Guide us, Lord, and teach us Your ways. Amen."

❧

*This is unbelievable. Who ever heard of a pastor that mows the church lawn? He could have told me who he was, but he led me to think...*

Carin's thoughts were interrupted by the crescendo of the keyboard. As she bowed her head and listened to the sincerity of Jake's prayer, her indignation quickly grew into a grudging respect. He had a gentle calmness about him, and his faith was evident in both the words he shared and the tone of his voice. She breathed deeply and allowed herself to relax, letting the words flow over her. The nervousness that had nearly paralyzed her as she entered the church diminished. It had been so long since she'd worshiped like this, too long since her prayers had been anything but mechanical—if she said any prayers at all—that she felt like a sponge soaking up water.

No lightning strikes from above—yet. *Maybe it really is true...what the Bible says about the Living Water.* With each word, Carin felt fissures weaken the concrete wall that bound her heart like an airtight vault.

It was easy to see how she'd missed the fact Jake was a pastor. He didn't look like any pastor she'd ever seen. He was dressed in neatly pressed khakis that seemed tailor-made for his long, lean legs and a navy jacket over a tan button-down shirt that covered a broad expanse of shoulders. No tie, no robe, no collar. Weren't all pastors supposed to wear a robe or collar or *something* to set them apart from everyone else while they preached? And he wasn't any older than she was. Weren't all senior pastors just this side of old and gray?

She remembered the way he'd looked while they spoke in the churchyard on Friday afternoon, handsome in a rugged sort of way, his dark hair speckled with grass that had caught in the tousled waves. He was nearly a foot taller than her petite five feet, three inches, and his tanned skin glistened from exertion where it wasn't covered by a grass-splattered T-shirt and faded jeans.

Beside her, Corey's knee pumped like a piston. He threw her nervous sidelong glances as Jake wound his way through the sermon. Carin wondered if Corey heard a word his brother said. His lack of attention didn't only apply to the classroom, she imagined.

As they sang the closing hymn, Corey scooted away from her, clearly anticipating a quick escape. But Jake kept an eagle eye on him. When the music faded and people began to gravitate toward the exit, Jake motioned to Corey with a slight nod of his head and a stern look.

"Oh, brother." Corey grimaced and turned back to Carin. His blue eyes narrowed as he sighed in resignation. "Jake wants me to take you to his office. I guess I'm in hot water now."

"Scalding." Carin gathered her purse and slipped the strap over her shoulder. "Although I don't think you're the only one who has explaining to do."

*That* piqued his interest. "What do you mean?"

"I can see where you get your mischievous bent." She nodded toward Jake. "The apple doesn't fall far from the tree, so to speak."

"That's a figure of speech, isn't it?"

"Exactly. Maybe you do listen in class—*occasionally*."

"Are you trying to ruin my life more than it already is?"

"What's that supposed to mean?"

"When you're through talking to him, Jake's gonna ground me forever."

"You should have thought of that *before* you hid my green pens on the shelf behind the dictionaries and turned in blank assignments with silly little drawings scrawled across the paper." She crossed her arms. "And how about the plastic mouse in my desk drawer?"

"How do you know *I'm* the one who did that?"

"I have my ways and you, Corey Samuels, have way too much time on your hands."

"I've been framed."

"Tell it to your brother. Maybe *he'll* believe you."

"Sure, he will." Corey buried his head in his hands and groaned. "I'm doomed."

# 4

Jake watched Corey and Carin slip from their seats. As Corey slinked by, grumbling, Jake struggled to remain focused on a story Mr. Doran was sharing.

"Want a soda or some cookies?" Corey's voice drifted as he and Carin wound their way into the hallway.

"If you're trying to butter me up, it's too late," Carin replied. "Besides, flowers work better than soda."

Corey shrugged. "I don't know anything about flowers, but I know where Jake hides a stash of soda. Might as well take the edge off your appetite. He'll be a while. It's never an easy getaway for him on Sunday mornings. You wouldn't believe half the stuff people hang around to tell him."

Jake cringed. Corey's mouth had no filter, and often his flippant comments left a mess for Jake to clean up. The last thing he wanted was for Carin to think he wasn't serious about his pastoral duties. It was the farthest thing from the truth. And besides, what kind of message would that send?

"Oh, I think I would." Carin struggled to keep up with Corey. Her sandals clacked over the tile floor. "But a soda sounds good."

Corey disappeared into a small kitchen off the main hallway, reappearing moments later with a bag of chocolate-crème cookies and two cans of soda.

Jake listened in stereo—one ear funneling Mr. Doran's anecdote while the other zoned in on Corey. He was becoming an expert at multi-tasking when it came to detouring Corey from mischief.

"The breakfast of champions." Corey held up the goods like a prizefighter as he led Carin to Jake's office. When they passed by, his voice carried. "I'll share if you promise not to tattle to Jake. He doesn't like me eating junk food for breakfast."

The glib comment sent Jake over the edge. He nodded to Mr. Doran, and then politely interrupted the man when he paused for a breath. "Excuse me, but I have to go. Corey needs me."

Mr. Doran smiled his gap-toothed grin and shook Jake's hand, unaffected by the sudden departure, yet Jake felt torn as he strode down the hall. How many times had he had to choose between doing his job and bailing Corey out of trouble? The struggle was wearing on him. He paused outside the door and gathered his patience as he peeked in and listened to the voices that drifted.

"It's not exactly breakfast, since it's after eleven." Carin popped the top off the soda can before drawing a sip. "But I really should tell your brother, after the way you've been behaving in English class." She paced the room, frowning. "Or maybe we can negotiate, write up a behavioral contract. Oh, wait! Apparently I've forgotten my famous green *slasher* pen."

Her censuring look speared Corey. "This can't be happening." He groaned and hung his head. "Oh, God, help me."

Jake pushed the door wide and strode into the room. "I believe He's the only one who can."

"Uh-oh." Corey froze mid-stride. He fingered the tab on his soda, and then thrust the unopened can at Jake. "Want it?"

"No, thanks." Jake pushed the can back and crossed the room to greet Carin. "Hello again. I don't believe we've properly met." He grasped her hand, noting skin that was cool and smooth. Again, Jake noticed the scent of sandalwood...a fragrance that was quickly becoming familiar. "I'm Jake— *Pastor* Jake Samuels. And you are..."

"She's Miss O'Malley, my English teacher." Corey slumped against the couch and set the can of soda on the side table. "Remember I told you about her?"

"Ah...so this is the infamous Slasher." Jake released her

hand to wiggle from his suit jacket and drape it over the back of his desk chair. "I'm pleased to see you again, Miss O'Malley. Corey *did* tell me a bit about you."

"Apparently he has." Her irritated gaze faltered. She smoothed the hand he'd grasped with her other, soothing as if his touch had scorched. "I...you..."

"What's the matter?" Suddenly the room felt unbearably warm. Jake turned to check the thermostat, adjusted the air a few degrees cooler. "You never imagined the thirsty lawnmower guy baking in the blistering afternoon sun could be the pastor you were in such hot pursuit of on Friday?"

"Obviously not." Carin sighed as the air kicked on, rushing over her from the vent above. Jake watched her hair flutter, and she smoothed it with one hand, tucking the strands behind her ear. "I stand corrected."

"Well, now that we've got that cleared up...Corey, drop the stash of cookies and take a seat at the table so we can talk."

"No, thanks." Corey shook his head. "You two are doing just fine, Jake. Maybe I should leave and let you hash things out. Just call me when the fireworks are over."

"It's not up for debate." The tone of Jake's voice spurred Corey to release the bag of cookies and double-time it to the little round table. Jake pulled a chair for Carin and motioned for her to join Corey. Then he closed the office door and settled into a chair as well.

The three sat, surrounded by awkward silence as the air conditioning *whooshed*. Corey fidgeted and tugged at the collar of his navy polo shirt. "Well, are we gonna talk or what?"

Carin shifted in her seat. "You're a wonderful speaker, Jake," she offered. "That was a beautiful service. It really moved me."

"Where to?" Corey released his collar and rocked back in his chair. His gaze, tinged with a bit of defiance, locked with Carin's.

"Not funny." Jake pushed Corey's chair back toward the table until all four legs clattered against the tile. "Sit up."

"Sorry." Corey straightened in the seat. "I couldn't help

myself."

"Apparently Corey often can't help himself," Carin interjected as she turned to address Jake. "In pranks and disruptions, your brother definitely gets an A-plus. He's outstanding. He could teach a college honors class on the subject of delaying instruction. Pure genius."

"That good at it?" Jake's mood darkened to thunderstorm status. "Hmmm, go on."

"On the other hand, in grammar and writing he can use more than a little practice."

"I gather he's not bound for the honor roll?"

"Not even close, at the rate he's going." Carin pulled a folded sheet of computer paper from her purse. "Here's a print out of Corey's English grades for the first grading period so far." The paper rattled as she unfolded it then dropped it on the table and slid it toward Jake. "As you can see, Corey's quickly slipping into the abyss of failure."

"An F?" Corey sat up and snatched the paper. "There's no way. It has to be a mistake. I've never made an F."

"Let me see that." Jake took it and scanned the print. His voice was strained, his patience tattered. "It says so right here, Corey. You have two missing assignments and a failing grade on last week's Chapter Two test."

"There's no mistake," Carin said firmly. "And the most disappointing thing is I know you can do better, Corey. You know you can, too."

"This isn't fair. You ambushed me!" Corey's chair toppled as he leapt up. "It's Sunday, for crying out loud. Who has a school conference on Sunday?"

"We do. We are." Carin's voice maintained calm as Corey huffed, pacing the room. Jake imagined that in teaching middle school she'd had a lot of practice with defiant kids. He, on the other hand, felt his patience snap like a worn rubber band.

"Enough." Jake reached for the chair Corey had toppled and righted it, setting it down hard. "Corey, you will sit down, lower your voice, and show respect to Miss O'Malley."

"But—"

"Now."

Corey paused a moment, and Jake knew he was debating his options. Finding none favorable, he expelled a heavy breath and wilted back into the chair. He hid his eyes beneath a fan of dark hair and crossed his arms tight over his chest.

Jake started a silent count toward ten.

"Corey, I'm here because you are my student, and I care about you." Carin leaned in to murmur. Her voice was low and coaxing, yet filled with resolve. "We both have a long year ahead of us, so we need to work together. I want to help you."

Corey slouched in the seat and turned away, his cheeks flushed. "Why do you care?"

The question seemed to startle Carin. "Does it matter?"

Her gaze faltered as Corey's eyes filled with tears, startling Jake, as well. He'd seen all sorts of reactions from Corey in the past—sulking, arguing, stomping away to slam a door—but the crying jag was something new. Maybe it was a breakthrough of some sort.

"Yes." Corey swiped the tears away, scowling. "Shouldn't it?"

"I suppose so." Carin reached over to brush damp hair from Corey's forehead, and Jake's breath caught at the tender gesture. He realized just how long it had been since Corey had felt the comforting touch of their mom. He coughed to dislodge the lump that filled his throat.

"So..." Corey challenged.

Carin settled her hands in her lap and drew a breath. "Corey, you have the capability to be an amazing writer."

"Doesn't matter." Corey's voice stabbed, but his eyes widened slightly at the compliment. He sniffled, and Jake sensed he struggled to keep the tears from his voice. "I like football, and baseball, too. English is a waste of time. Who cares if a word is a dangling participle or the object of a preposition?"

"I care, and you should, too." She drummed delicate fingers on the tabletop. "Besides, I'm not talking about grammar. I'm talking about writing. It's a way to express yourself, to communicate with others. And grammar is the foundation of all writing—like block work is the foundation of a building. Good writing can open doors to so many things, Corey."

"I can open my own doors." Corey shrugged. "Besides, I'm gonna play football. That's the only door I want to open."

"And you can shine above all the other good players with your writing," Carin insisted. "Especially when you're filling out college applications or corresponding with scouts—or an agent—should it come to that, eventually. You have to trust me on this."

His eyes filled with tears again. "Why should I trust you?"

"Because I have a plan." She tossed a look at Jake. "Providing you agree, Jake."

"Here we go," Corey swiped his eyes and slouched low in the chair. "Write, write, and write some more. I hope you have a huge stash of pens, 'cause you're gonna need them."

Carin ignored the sarcasm and continued, turning her attention to Jake. "As Corey knows, I'm the sponsor of the student newspaper at East Ridge Middle. It's a good newspaper, but it can be better. I'm looking for co-editors, two students who can be taught to gather information and write lead stories. I've already spoken with one student about helping to move things in a new direction, and she's agreed. Now, if Corey would just hop on board, I know he'd be perfect for the job as well."

"Me? Are you crazy?"

"Corey!" Jake glared at him. "Check the attitude."

"But she wants me to work with a girl, Jake." He slapped the thighs of his khakis, and Jake noticed a new rip at the knee. He grimaced as Corey continued. "The guys will laugh me right off the football team."

"Nonsense. They'll do no such thing." The last of Jake's patience snapped.

"Boy, are you out of the loop." Corey wiggled his thumb

into the hole at his knee, tearing the fabric even more.

"Consider it penance, then, for your insufferable behavior." Jake wagged a finger sharply. "It's got to stop, Corey. And I mean, now."

"That's a stiff penalty." Corey swiped his nose with the back of his hand. He flipped hair from his eyes and scowled at Carin. "Who is the girl—the one you want me to work with?"

"Amy MacGregor."

"No way." Corey stiffened in the chair. "Anyone but her. She's a know-it-all. It's not fair. I won't do it."

"That's fine." Jake's voice remained cool, though his temper reached red alert. "We'll use the time you practice for football as study time instead. Straight home from school each afternoon. No game. I'm sure Coach McCrosky would agree once he gets a look at your grades."

"What? No!"

"There's one more thing," Carin broke in, as if she hadn't heard Corey's objections. "I want you to keep a journal and write at least a page every day."

"What? Why?"

"Because, you have to actually *do* some writing in order to *improve* your writing skills. *And* if you write each day, and turn your journal in, I'll count the journal entries toward credit for those two essays you failed to complete. You still have to finish the grammar pages you missed, though, and retake the chapter test you failed to study for."

"This is bad…" Corey groaned. "I don't want to keep a journal, and I don't want to work on the paper with—with Amy MacGregor."

"Settle down before you give yourself a stroke," Jake admonished. "Miss O'Malley's requests are more than reasonable…and very generous."

"But—"

"You made your bed, now—"

"I know…sleep in it."

"*Lie* in it," Carin corrected.

"Whatever." Corey raked a hand through his hair. "Oh, I

despise figures of speech."

Jake tapped his fingers along the table. "I consider this issue settled." He opened a file drawer at his desk. "Just so happens I have an extra notebook right here, perfect for a journal. You can write your first entry today, Corey, and be on the road to hauling your English grade right out of that abyss of failure."

Corey's gaze narrowed. "And if I decide to run away instead?"

"Consider the consequences."

"That's what you always say." Corey gritted his teeth and sighed as if the world was in its final hours. "I'll do it, but I don't have to like it."

"No, you don't have to like it at all," Jake agreed. "But you'll do a good job, regardless, because you don't want to revisit this topic." His tone left no room for argument. "Do I make myself clear?"

"Crystal." Corey tossed the notebook onto the table. "Can I go now? Dillon's parents are waiting to take me to that ballgame."

"*May* I. And you can go as soon as you've finished writing a page—or more—in your journal." Jake gathered the notebook and handed it to him once more.

"What am I supposed to write about?"

"Anything," Carin explained. She reached into her purse and found a pen. "Anything at all."

❧

Jake sipped sweet tea at the kitchen table as he poured over his planner, making notes in the schedule for the week ahead. A blood drive with the local donor bank was slated for Tuesday, and Mrs. Jenkins was scheduled for a hip replacement on Wednesday morning. The sweet older woman was nervous beyond words, so he'd promised to sit with her pre-op and wait through the surgery, covering her with prayer. Afterwards, he'd head back to the church to meet with the trustee committee to work through finalizing plans for the playground improvement project. And tomorrow he had a planning meeting with Patrick to hash out details for a youth outing to a local amusement park.

*I'm covered up until Thursday…again.*

Jake sighed as the front door slammed, signaling Corey's arrival home from the ball game. He bounded into the room and went straight to the refrigerator as if he hadn't just spent the last several hours plowing through hot dogs, nachos, and overstuffed bags of buttery popcorn.

"Hey." Corey nodded as he grabbed a gallon jug of milk from the refrigerator door. "What's up?" He twisted off the lid and guzzled straight from the container.

"Don't do that. Get a glass," Jake scolded.

"Oops, sorry. I forgot." Corey spun to grab a glass from the dish drain. He filled it to the brim then launched an assault on the pantry. A bag of cookies and a container of microwavable macaroni and cheese filled his arms when he turned back to Jake.

"How was the game?"

"Incredible. We had lower-bowl seats, so I could follow every play."

"Good. And I see Patrick and Julie starved you while you were at the ball field."

"Nah. I had two chili dogs and one of those giant, soft pretzels dipped in cheese. Oh, and Dillon and I shared a bag of salted peanuts."

"Just listening to you makes my gut twist in agony."

"Not me. I'm still hungry." As if to emphasize the point, Corey delved into the bag of cookies and brought out a pair. He popped the first into his mouth, and then twisted one chocolate side from the second to scrape creamy white filling with his teeth.

Jake closed his planner and leaned back in the chair. He tapped the table with one hand while he motioned Corey to join him. "While you're eating your way through the next five courses, have a seat and let's talk."

"I can talk standing up." Corey's voice was garbled through a mouthful of cookie. He washed the crumbs down with a swig of milk.

"I said sit."

"Oh, brother, here it comes. Not the lecture…anything but the lecture." Corey slouched into a chair, crossed his arms, and feigned a look of total disinterest as his hand disappeared into the cookie bag again. "Besides, you've already lectured me today. There ought to be a quota."

"I'll cut to the chase." Jake leveled a look. "The honeymoon's over, Corey. I allowed you some slack last spring, because of the accident and the fact that you came to a new school so late in the year. But now you have a fresh start, a clean slate, and you've had a chance to heal—"

"At least on the outside, right?"

"Guilt won't work anymore, Corey." Jake struggled to keep his tone firm, though he wanted to draw Corey into his arms and soothe away the hurt. That would do neither of them any good now. "You can't make excuses forever. We have to move on. *You* have to move on. So, either show improvement in your schoolwork beginning right now—today—or you're off the football team. It's your choice. No more chances. End of discussion. Is that totally clear?"

Corey dropped the bag of cookies and crossed his arms. "I heard you when you said it the first time, in your office this morning, with Miss O'Malley."

"Good." Jake tapped his pencil against the cover of his planner. "It was nice of her to come out to the church to help you."

"You mean filet me…and then grill me."

"Don't be so melodramatic." Jake shook his head. "She seems nice…and caring."

Corey leaned back in the chair, balancing on only two legs. "Don't get any ideas."

"What do you mean?"

"I know that look. You had it with Rachelle before I came along to mess things up for you."

"You didn't mess up anything, Corey. What happened with Rachelle wasn't your fault."

"She didn't like me."

"It wasn't you, Corey. It was…" Jake sighed. How could he explain? "Maybe you should get a head start on your journal for tomorrow."

Corey let the chair slip forward again. The front legs clattered to the tile. "You're no fun anymore, Jake. All you do is boss me around."

Jake's heart tore at the comment, and he struggled to keep his voice steady. "I'm not bossing you. I'm just stating the facts."

"It wasn't like this…with Mom and Dad." Corey's voice caught, and Jake wondered if he might break down and cry again. "It was easy."

"It will get easier again, Corey. Trust me."

"You said God doesn't make mistakes." Corey's lower lip trembled, and suddenly he looked a whole lot younger than twelve. He rubbed his eyes, fought back a sniffle and turned his face away from Jake. "But He took Mom and Dad, and that has to be a mistake, doesn't it?"

"Sometimes we don't understand right away why things happen." Hadn't Jake asked himself the same question a hundred times over? The answer was always the same. "Sometimes we never understand. But that doesn't mean those things are mistakes."

"So you think it was right for Mom and Dad to…to die?"

"I didn't say that. I just said—"

"I don't want to talk about it." Corey pushed back from the table. "I'm going to bed."

"Corey, wait." Jake reached for him. "We should talk this out."

"I'm tired, Jake. And I'm not hungry anymore." Corey wiggled from Jake's grasp and looked at him with damp, wounded eyes. He opened his mouth to speak but clamped it shut before uttering a word. Instead, he grabbed the bag of cookies and the mac-and-cheese and tossed them back into the pantry. "See you in the morning."

"Goodnight." Filled with a sense of helplessness, Jake watched him lope through the doorway and into the hall.

"Whatever." Corey's voice drifted back.

Jake pressed a hand to his throbbing forehead and wished he could banish the offensive word from the English language, forever. A door slammed, and the springs on Corey's bed squeaked in protest beneath his weight. Then oppressive silence blanketed the house.

*How will I ever reach him? I miss my brother…the happy-go-lucky kid he used to be.* Jake stood and stretched his legs. He refilled his glass with sweet tea and wandered out to the back porch to collapse into a padded rattan chair. The night was unseasonably warm—an Indian summer—but the musky scent of fall clung to the air. The sky was a swatch of black velvet dotted by sparkling sequins, and in the distance, cicadas sang a melancholy tune. Jake sipped tea and allowed his mind to wander to thoughts of Carin O'Malley.

After their meeting, he'd walked her to her car while Corey sulked over the journal. The breeze was warm beneath a brilliant sun, and the lot was deserted except for his Jeep, her powder-blue sedan, and the van Patrick and Julie used to haul their brood.

"Thanks for taking the time to come today." Jake paused as they reached the car. He leaned against the bumper and turned his face to the sun. "I'm sorry Corey's been so much trouble."

"It will be better now." Carin's voice soothed his worry. She smiled and tucked a strand of hair behind one ear as the breeze freed it from a silver clip.

"I sure hope so." Jake cleared his throat, trying to focus on Corey instead of the sandalwood scent that clung to Carin's skin.

"I *know* so. I have a sixth sense about these things."

Jake shifted his weight against the rear fender. "So, you've done this before?"

"I…" She paused, bit her lower lip, and then seemed to

shift gears. "What middle school teacher hasn't?"

"Hmm…" He thought for a moment. "Most of them?"

She shrugged. "The ones I know go the extra mile."

"Well, I'm thankful for you. As you can guess, Corey needs something that, so far, I haven't been able to give him."

"What happened to Corey?"

"Not just Corey…us." Jake lowered his voice. "My folks— our folks—died last January."

"I'm so sorry, Jake." Her eyes flashed with shock, then narrowed. Jake caught a glimpse of tears as she dipped her head and turned slightly. "But that…explains things."

"We're just trying to get our bearings. It's taking longer than I expected."

He watched her swipe a tear from one eye with the tip of her finger.

"Well, I'll help as much as I can from my end." Her voice was thick, the southern lilt more defined.

"I appreciate it." Jake jammed his hands into his pockets. "And I'm sorry about the…confusion."

"You mean the caretaker thing?" She shrugged slightly.

"Yeah, that."

"No harm done." She turned back to him and wiggled one foot, clad in a strappy sandal. "I still have all my toes."

Jake laughed and opened the car door for her. "I guess I'll be seeing you?"

"I'll keep you posted…on Corey's progress, I mean." She slipped into the driver's seat and reached for a tissue from a box on the console. "It was nice to meet you, Jake."

"I'm here every Sunday and plenty in between."

"I'll keep that in mind." She dabbed her eyes, then offered a slight smile as she slipped a key into the ignition. "See you soon."

A barking dog a few yards down drew Jake back. He sipped tea and pictured Carin sitting on her own back porch, grading papers with one of her infamous green pens, as she twirled a strand of sleek curls around a finger. Maybe between papers she paused to gaze up at the same starlit sky he admired.

*Does it look the same to her...like an ocean of wishes just beyond reach?*

Maybe he'd pay her a visit later this week...check up on Corey's progress. Jake smiled at the thought and drained his glass. He leaned back in the chair, propped his hands behind his head, and sighed.

# 5

"So this is your battleground?" Jake leaned in the doorway to survey the seventh grade classroom. Oversized paperback dictionaries were stacked in neat piles along a bookshelf on the far wall, and workbook pages filled colorful file bins beneath a window that ushered in brilliant afternoon sun. Carin's neat handwriting graced one side of the dry-erase board with a list of this week's vocabulary words. The letters were printed with a flourish, and on the far side of the board, she'd outlined the steps to a well-constructed essay.

"Hello, Jake." Carin looked up from a desk covered in a sea of essays, and Jake's breath caught at the way sunlight danced across her eyes, bringing out a deeper shade of emerald. Her hair hung loose today—soft curls kissed the nape of her neck and brushed across her forehead. She clutched a green pen in one hand. Jake laughed, and she scrunched her nose at him. "What's so funny?"

"I'm...um...just admiring your weapon of choice."

She followed his gaze and then laughed softly, too, as she loosened her grip on the pen. "I just bought a new pack, wore the last one out. The writing's improving by leaps and bounds, though, so all my efforts with the students seem to be paying off."

"Does that include Corey?"

"Well, so far he's turned in his journal this week, and he retook that chapter test—made an A, I might add—so he's on the right track. And he did a better job on the essay I assigned yesterday. Would you like to see?"

"May I?"

"Of course. It was a free-write activity, and each student

got to choose his or her topic of choice." She thumbed through the pile and handed a dog-eared sheet of notebook paper to Jake. "Corey wrote about you."

"He did?" Jake glanced at the title and frowned. "'My Brother's Most Annoying Habits.' Wow, I'll bet this was entertaining to read. Let's see…'Tells me not to drink out of the milk carton—who cares? Nobody else drinks out of it but me. Won't let me go to the arcade on Friday nights—*everyone* goes to the arcade on Friday night. Makes me do my homework on Friday night instead of going to the arcade—do I really have to elaborate on this one?'" Jake grimaced. "I sound like a real dictator, don't I?"

"Just your typical walk through parenthood."

"But I'm *not* his parent. I'm just his brother. Sometimes I really miss just being his brother. It was a whole lot easier and definitely more fun."

"I'm sorry, Jake."

"But on the bright side, he only got, let's see…" Jake smoothed his index finger across the paper, counting the green marks. "Four slashes and two comments. Not bad for a two-page essay." He handed the paper back to Carin and eased over to a student desk. He pulled the chair back. "May I?"

"I'm not sure you'll fit, but give it a try."

"Funny thing"—Jake settled in, though his knees were seriously cramped in the minimal space beneath the desk—"but I don't remember any of my teachers looking quite like…you."

"What, no green pens?" Carin waggled the tip at him.

He laughed. "I mean…well…"

"Cat got your tongue?"

He grimaced, suddenly wondering what he was thinking here, stumbling around asking her for a date. After the debacle with Rachelle, he'd sworn off women, hadn't he? Yet something drew him to Carin…something he couldn't explain. He shifted his weight in the desk, bumped his knees against the wood and grimaced as a jolt of pain shot through him. "I'm with Corey. Those figures of speech…"

"A little extra homework can help with that."

"Give me a minute here. I think I'm a bit oxygen deprived in…this…cramped…space." He shifted again, freeing his legs. "That's better." He trained his gaze on her deep green eyes. "Now, what I'd really like is dinner with you—to say thank you for all you're doing to help Corey, and, well…because I'd like to have dinner with you."

"Oh. In that case…"

Jake plunged right in, no turning back now. "Do you like Chinese food?"

"Yes. Very much."

"It's short notice, but Corey's over at Dillon's working on a science project, and I know this little place just down the road…"

"Oh, tonight?" The smile melted from Carin's face. "I'd love to, Jake, but I already have plans."

"Should have figured that." Jake felt an odd sense of disappointment. "Well, would you mind giving me your number so I can call you? My schedule's kind of crazy, but I'm sure we can work something out…in this millennium."

"I…" She hesitated, then shook her head and laughed nervously. "I guess it would be OK."

"I'm not trying to force you into anything. No pressure, OK?" Jake leaned back in the chair. "Tell you what. Why don't you come out to the church on Saturday morning with Hailey and help with the playground improvements and the garden area? She's getting a group together, and I'm at the top of the list."

"She mentioned that and asked me to help, too."

"So, what's the verdict?"

"I'll think about it." Carin shuffled the papers on her desk, and Jake wondered if she felt the same odd flutter in her belly that he did.

She looked up at him. "Now, you should unfold yourself from that desk before you suffer permanent damage, and I really need to finish these essays before I leave. I don't want to take work home tonight."

"I guess I'll go, then." Jake stood up, massaging a cramp from his right leg. He pushed the chair in. "Thanks again for helping Corey. I hope to see you again…soon."

෧෴෧

"Was that Pastor Jake I saw leaving your classroom?" Hailey asked as she paused at Carin's classroom doorway with her purse slung over one shoulder and a paper-filled tote in hand.

"Yes. He stopped by to check on Corey."

"How's that situation going?"

"Better…so far."

Hailey leaned one hip against the doorjamb. "Did I hear him ask you to dinner?"

"Were you eavesdropping?"

"Me?" Her hazel eyes widened and she shook her head. "No. I just happened to be passing by when he mentioned something about you, him, and a Chinese restaurant. So, are you going to go?"

"I told him I have plans."

"You—what plans?"

"My usual Thursday evening plans…you know." Carin checked her watch and gasped. "Oh, and I'm late. Gotta go." She gathered the tote and her cotton sweater.

"Carin, wait." Hailey followed as Carin pushed past her to rush down the hall. "If Jake asks again, you should go to dinner with him. He's a nice guy."

"He's a pastor. If he knew what I've been through—the whole story—he wouldn't have anything to do with me. Nothing at all."

"You have to quit thinking like that. It's not true."

"It *is* true."

"Have you gotten any more calls from you-know-who?"

The mention of Phillip caused Carin's belly to tumble. "A few nights ago. But I can't talk about it now. I don't *want* to talk about it now. I'll call you later."

"You'd better. And I want to chat with you about helping with that grounds-keeping project at church. It would be good for you to get out and meet some new people...people under the age of eighty, at least."

"Later, Hailey. I have to go. Lilly's waiting for me. I promised her a special dinner tonight."

Carin practically flew to her car. She made a quick stop at the Chuck's Fried Chicken drive-thru on her way to the senior center. The brown-brick building flanked by a flowing creek at the edge of town was becoming more familiar with each passing week. Leaves on the maple trees that lined a concrete walkway were beginning to change to subtle hues of yellow and orange laced with magenta. Double glass doors swished open and the odor inside swirled around her—a mixture of disinfectant and age mingled with food from the cafeteria.

Carin had been visiting at the center for nearly three months, and she didn't know who enjoyed the visits more— her or Lilly. She'd been hooked since she saw a news segment on the evening edition of Channel Ten News. The local nursing home was looking for volunteers to visit with their residents—kind of a reverse Big Brother/Big Sister program. So one day after school Carin went to inquire, and she was matched with Lilly. Now she visited for a few hours every Thursday evening.

She knocked on the door of a room farthest down the first-floor hall, and then entered without waiting for a response. The scent of spearmint greeted her—Lilly grew the aromatic plant in a box on the sill of her large picture window that overlooked an expansive, serene pond—and she enjoyed chewing the leaves in lieu of gum.

"Hello, Lilly." Carin smiled at the slight woman with a shock of white hair pulled back into a neat chignon. She sat in a padded rocking chair beneath a tall floor lamp, reading a large-print paperback. "I brought you dinner."

"Hello, dear." Lilly glanced up and set the book aside. "How was school today?"

"An adventure, as usual." Carin set the paper bag filled

with Lilly's favorite chicken on the small side table. "But I'm beginning to get the hang of the routine."

"That's good. And that boy...the one who's been giving you so much trouble?"

"Corey." Carin found a glass in the cabinet and poured Lilly sweet tea. "I talked to his brother, and he's doing better."

"You spoke with his brother?" Lilly's eyes narrowed behind wire-rimmed reading glasses. "But where are his parents?"

"They died...in an accident. I don't know the details."

"You should find out, dear." Lilly took the glass Carin offered, drew a sip, and smacked her lips loudly. "It might help."

"Maybe I will. His brother is the pastor of East Ridge Church."

"Pastor...of a church, you said?"

"Yes. I visited there last Sunday, and it was nice." Carin gazed out the picture window, to the graceful fountain in the center of an ample pond. Water arced in a fine spray, casting a mist into the air. Weeping willows danced in the breeze, their fine, wispy branches like ballerinas swaying in unison to a silent symphony. Ripples of water shimmered beneath waning sunlight. Carin's pulse eased as she drew a deep breath. Gazing at the pond always seemed to calm her.

"Then you should go again this week, Carin. You should go back to church."

"I don't know." A cardinal swooped from a willow to rest on the ground peppered by leaves. The crimson color stood out like a splash of blood. "I...can't, Lilly...not yet."

"Oh, don't let that man...what he did was wrong, oh, so wrong—"

*I should have never told her. It was a mistake to burden her with the dirty secrets in my life. I'm supposed to be here for her, not the other way around.* Yet Carin had needed someone to talk to, and Lilly was a good listener. The elderly woman had been a teacher for over thirty years, so their bond had been strong from the beginning. And somehow, Lilly had a way of drawing things from Carin that she was loathe to share with anyone else.

"I don't want to talk about it." Carin lifted a crocheted baby cap from the basket at Lilly's feet. "This is a pretty shade of pink." The cap was tiny—just the right size for a newborn's delicate head. "How many caps did you crochet this week?"

"I'm not sure. Would you count them for me?"

"Of course." As Carin counted, she separated the caps into stacks of baby blue and soft pink. "Nine, so far. How do you do it, Lilly?"

"The good Lord guides me, and the exercise chases arthritis away." She massaged the gnarled knuckles of her mottled hands. "I might be able to crank out a few more before the hospital volunteer stops by to pick them up in the morning."

"I'll help, if you like," Carin offered. "You can teach me the stitches after we eat. Do you think I can learn how to crochet, too?"

"Of course you can learn." Lilly smiled and patted a canvas bag full of colorful skeins. "We'll go step by step and do it together." She delved into the bag. "I think there's another hook in here."

Lilly crocheted the caps for the Neonatal Intensive Care Unit at Children's Hospital as a gift for each baby who was admitted following birth. She said a prayer over each cap as she tied the final stitch, and confided in Carin that she hoped each brought a special blessing to the infant who wore it.

"Are you hungry, Lilly?" Carin took chicken and mashed potatoes with brown gravy, warm and steaming, from the to-go container and arranged a helping for each of them on plates she took from one of Lilly's cabinets. "We should eat before the chicken gets cold."

"Chicken?" The older woman's eyes glazed over, and Carin's heart sank at the faraway look that was becoming all too familiar. "OK, Elise. But we really should wait for your father. He'll be home from work soon."

Carin's heart lurched. This was the main reason Lilly and

Carin had been matched. The counselors thought more conversation might keep her brain alert and stave off the effects of the Alzheimer's, at least for a while. Sometimes it seemed to be working, but other times…

"Lilly," Carin busied her hands, removing foil cartons from the white to-go bag. "I'm not Elise. I'm Carin."

"Carin? Where's your father, Elise? He should be home from work by now."

Carin patted the older woman's shoulder. The counselor had said it was best not to reason with her, as that only agitated her further. "It's OK…" Carin's throat felt stuffed with cotton as tears burned her eyes. She forced her voice to steady. "How about we take a walk to the pond while we wait? The food will keep and we can take the yarn with us to crochet another cap. The babies need them."

𝒶𝓈

Jake checked his watch as he slipped past the receptionist's desk and down the hall of the senior center. Good thing Patrick's distress call had come in as Jake neared the center, or he might not have had time to make the visit before he was due to pick up Corey from football practice.

Pastor Julian, a resident at the senior center, was agitated again, and the only thing that seemed to calm him was a visit from Jake. When Pastor Julian lost his ability to walk following a fall that broke his hip, he was moved to a new room in a higher-level-care section of the center. The change had caused a turn for the worse. The doctors told Jake it was just a matter of time. The poor man's body was simply worn out. Jake forced the thought from his mind.

As Jake wound his way down the long hall to the last room on the left, he reflected on how they'd met during a youth event nearly two years ago, when he, Patrick, and Julie brought a group of kids to sing in the community room. Pastor Julian had been the first to arrive for the singing and the last to leave, and Jake had helped him back to his room, taking him by one arm while he leaned heavily on his cane with the other.

Back then, Pastor Julian's body was weakened by the progression of time, but his mind was sharp. Oh, the stories they shared over the weeks and months that followed! Pastor Julian had ministered to a series of little country churches for nearly sixty years, and Jake found himself fascinated by the rich history in simple reflections of a life well lived. What Jake had thought would be nothing more than a passing community service event for the youth had grown into a deep friendship. Jake assumed he'd counsel Pastor Julian, but in the end, the reverse was actually true—over the months Pastor Julian had become his anchor in a sea of chaos.

But Pastor Julian had begun to have episodes of confusion due to the onset of Alzheimer's. And these episodes took the life from him, like a leech slowly sucking away bits and pieces of what was good. Pastor Julian had been married to his high school sweetheart, Ava, for sixty-two years before a massive stroke claimed her a few winters ago. They had no children of their own, and Pastor Julian never elaborated as to why. But Jake quickly became the grandson Pastor Julian never had, and their bond grew as strong as the trunk of a solid old oak.

As Jake neared the end of the hall, he turned his attention to a burst of commotion. Something inside Pastor Julian's room—most likely the cane he still insisted he was capable of using— tumbled to the floor. Then the door swung wide, and a nurse let Jake in. Pastor Julian was sobbing. Big, sloppy tears covered his mottled face like a flowing river, wrenching Jake's heart. Jake went to the wheelchair, fell to his knees and slipped his hand into Pastor Julian's.

"Hey there." Jake stroked the man's callused fingers, and he relaxed almost immediately at the sound of Jake's voice. "What's the matter?"

"I smell the spearmint, Jake, and I see her."

"Ava?" A shiver snaked down Jake's spine. He smelled the strong scent of spearmint, too. How could that be?

"Yes." Pastor Julian tugged at Jake's shirt with his arthritic hand. "She's near the pond, and I have to go. She's waiting for me."

Jake turned his attention to the huge picture window that overlooked a large, tree-shaded pond beyond a black-topped walking trail. A pretty white gazebo stood at one end, its interior filled with bench seats. Majestic willows swayed in the breeze, their long, narrow leaves scattered across the water and along the bank. Pastor Julian liked to visit the pond, especially on warm fall days, and gaze at the water as leaves fluttered and danced along the surface. On occasion, he swore he saw Ava standing on the shore waiting for him.

Sometimes the pond was crowded with residents, most in wheelchairs or leaning on canes. Other times, it was deserted. Now he caught a glimpse of a woman with a shock of white hair. She sat in a chair with oversized wheels as she was pushed back toward the center by—

*Is that Carin?*

"Let's take a walk, Pastor Julian." Jake glanced at the nurse, and she nodded slightly. Then he reached for Pastor Julian's wire-framed glasses and slipped them over the older man's bulbous nose. "It's a nice evening to go down to the pond."

"Hurry, Jake." The man's arthritic hands trembled, but his voice filled with youthful enthusiasm. "I don't like to keep Ava waiting."

Jake felt the same measure of excitement as he gazed through the window, to the lithe woman with curls that danced on a breeze.

# 6

There was no football practice that Friday afternoon since the high school team used the field for a game, so Jake picked up Corey from school, and they headed to the greenway for a quick run. Running was something they'd gotten into together soon after Corey came to live with Jake. Corey had a lot of trouble sleeping, and when he did finally fall asleep each night, more often than not he was plagued by nightmares. So Jake had taken him to the pediatrician, who'd recommended running. They'd hit the greenway that same afternoon, and Corey slept through the night for the first time in weeks. Now they scheduled a run together at least twice a week.

"How's English class?" Jake asked as they slid into the second mile. The weather felt perfect for a long run—slightly cool and dry, with a mild breeze. The scent of mulched leaves filled the air with the musky scent of fall.

"OK. It's school." Corey breathed easily, as if taking a lazy summer stroll. Jake struggled to control his panting as his heart rate spiked.

"You fill up that journal yet?"

"I'm trying. It's not as hard as I thought it would be."

"Most things aren't."

"Miss O'Malley said I'm doing a lot better. She said to tell you...um...hi, too."

"Is that so?" Yesterday evening at the senior center, Carin and the ashen-haired woman in the wheelchair were gone by the time Jake made it to the pond with Pastor Julian. Now he wondered if he'd imagined the whole thing. He'd visited the center at least once a week for the past year and had never run into Carin there. So, what was she doing there now?

Finding his second wind, Jake picked up the pace. "Is that all Miss O'Malley said?"

"What else did you expect?" Corey matched him before edging into the lead then glanced back over his shoulder. "Oh, no. Hold up a minute. I know where this is headed. You're not gonna embarrass me and ask her out, are you?"

"I thought you prayed for me to find a girlfriend." Jake lengthened his stride and pushed a little harder, taking the lead back. "Change your mind?"

"No, but not *her*." Corey's legs pumped double-time to match Jake's pace. "Because that would be totally gross—you dating my teacher. I'd never survive it, so just wipe the idea from your mind."

"That bad, huh?" Jake frowned at him.

"Well, yeah." Corey jabbed a finger at his own throat and pretended to gag, all the while not breaking stride. "Just shoot me now, and get it over with."

"Not until I race you to the finish line." Jake motioned down the greenway, pointing out a stand of trees that marked the unofficial finish. "You're going to lose."

"Not today." Corey leaned into the breeze and pumped his arms harder.

"We'll see." Jake broke into a sprint. Corey's tennis shoes slapped the pavement as he adjusted his pace and worked to close the gap. They shared the lead until Jake burst ahead, just shy of the finish line. His longer stride gave him an edge, but it wouldn't last much longer. If Corey hit another growth spurt or two, he'd match Jake in height soon enough. Jake crossed the imaginary finish line and put on the brakes, doubling over to catch his breath. "Sorry, buddy, but you're gonna have to work harder than that if you want to beat me," he gasped.

"Just wait 'til next time." Corey leaned forward and sucked air. "I'm getting faster every week."

"True." Jake swiped sweat from his brow, urging his heart rate down a notch. "But so am I."

Corey was sure to sleep like a baby tonight. *Mission accomplished.*

When they both caught their breath and cooled a bit, they headed toward the Jeep. Sweat-soaked clothes clung to flushed skin.

Corey lifted the passenger door latch. "I edited the first two stories for the school newspaper this afternoon," he shared as he climbed into the seat.

"How'd it go?" Jake tugged off his sweatshirt, wiped his face in the cotton, and tossed the soiled shirt into the back seat of the Jeep before slipping into the driver's seat.

"It was awesome. Miss O'Malley gave me my own pack of orange pens. She said I can't use green, 'cause that's her own special color for slashing essays, but orange is even better, I think. It stands out more."

Jake laughed. "It does, huh?"

"Yeah. I got to rip apart Stu Bishop's story on the football homecoming game. He's such a wise—"

"Don't say it."

"Guy. I was gonna say guy."

"Sure, you were."

"Anyway, I felt the power. Rip, rip." Corey's hand slashed the air like a sword. "It was pretty cool."

"Sounds like Miss O'Malley may have unleashed a monster—Slasher Junior. Just don't let it go to your head."

"I won't."

"Famous last words." Jake cranked the engine. "Let's grab a quick shower and head to church. You have your guitar lesson tonight, and I've got some work to finish up before that groundskeeper's meeting tomorrow. Then we both need to hit the hay, because there's a lot of work to be done."

"There's always a lot of work to be done," Corey groaned. "But it gives me something to write about—besides you, that is."

"Yeah. We should talk about that—you using me for your essay fodder."

"I'm just following orders—write, write, write." Corey nodded. "Besides, I think Miss O'Malley likes reading about you."

"She does, huh?"

"Yeah. You're worth at least a B—usually an A."

Jake laughed and wondered if God had sent him Carin O'Malley for a reason he had yet to fully understand. The twist in his gut...the spike in his pulse...made Jake wonder if Corey's offhanded prayers really were being answered.

There was only one way to find out.

*∼∽*

Carin poured a cup of coffee and sat at the kitchen table. Scooter brushed up against her legs and she lifted him onto her lap and stroked his sleek, gray fur while he purred like a well-tuned engine. The scent of tuna from his food bowl wafted, and Carin wrinkled her nose. She wasn't a big fan of tuna.

Her cell phone sat in the center of the table, and she replayed the latest voicemail message in her mind as her heart raced.

"Carin." Phillip's smooth-as-honey business voice came over the line so clearly, that for a moment she froze with the fear he was standing right behind her. She could almost feel his hot breath burning her neck, as it had that awful night of Cameron's memorial service. A sob escaped her lips, because his speech was slurred, and she knew he was drunk—just like he was loaded that night, when he'd hurt her with his words...his actions. "I know you're listening to this. You should have never left Nashville...left me. Don't you know how much your leaving hurt me...and my chance to make Senior Partner? If you say a word to your father about what happened, you know what I'll do. You're just as guilty as I am. You know as well as I do that what happened was just as much your fault as mine. You made me crazy, Carin, and you ruined everything." He paused with a menacing sigh of frustration, and she pictured the storm in his gaze, the tight clench of his fists as he lifted them. "Fine, don't pick up so we can talk this through. I hope you sleep well tonight. Dream of me."

Carin tamped the urge to toss her phone into the trash. But instead, let the message replay just long enough to hit the delete button.

It made the fifth message this month—second this week. The calls were escalating. She should have known running away wouldn't make things go away, too. He'd always be able to find her…nothing would change that.

Carin drew a deep breath and forced tears back. Her cell phone chimed, startling her so her heart pummeled her ribs. She reached for the phone as if touching it might scald her and checked the caller ID.

She flipped open the phone and pressed it to her ear. "Dad?"

"Hi, honey. How are things there?"

Her voice caught, and suddenly tears pooled in her eyes. "Good…but I miss you."

"Are you OK? It sounds like you're crying."

"No. I just…" *Tell him,* her conscience battled. *No. He'll be crushed, and then his heart…*"It's just my friend, Lilly. When I went to visit last night, she had another episode."

"They seem to be increasing in frequency." Her father's voice was crowded with concern. "Do you really think it's wise for you to keep seeing her? Haven't you been through enough, losing your mom and then Cameron—both in such a short period of time?"

"You lost them, too."

"I know, but—"

"Most of the time Lilly's fine, and I really enjoy the visits." Carin struggled to steady her voice. "She's teaching me how to crochet so I can help her with the baby caps." She sniffled and brushed a tear from her eye. Guilt plagued her. It was wrong to lead him to think Lilly was the reason she was upset. *If he only knew the real reason.* "How's everything at the firm?"

"Busy as usual. I'm interviewing for another Senior Partner."

"Good. You need help, Dad. The doctor said you have to

lighten your load and rest more. You can't keep up the pace you've been pushing yourself to manage. It's dangerous."

"I'm still strong as an ox, so don't you fret, Carin. Let me do the worrying."

She sighed. There was no point in arguing with a seasoned attorney like Dad. "Well, are there any prospects for the position?"

"I've been considering Phillip, but he seems a bit...out of sorts lately." He cleared his throat. "I don't know what happened between the two of you, but—"

"I don't want to talk about it, Dad."

"Well, Phillip has always been my first choice. You know that, Carin. But I'm not sure your mom would feel the same."

"No?" This was a revelation. "Why not?"

"Nothing she could put her finger on. She just...had a feeling. You know how Mom was."

"Yes, I do." Carin's voice caught. "Why didn't she ever say anything to me?"

"Because you were in love with him, honey." Her dad paused. "*Are* you still in love with him?"

"No. I...don't want to talk about it." Carin dropped a tea bag into a cup and drowned it in boiling water from the teapot, then stirred in a spoonful of sugar as she watched it steep. "When are you coming for a visit, Dad?"

"I was about to ask you the same thing."

"I can't. I'm just settling into teaching here. I'm covered up in work." She had no desire to return to Nashville. There was a good chance she never would...if she could help it.

"Me, too."

"You should consider a vacation. Or you could come to East Ridge and stay with me for a while, and work from here. There's so much you can do over the Internet. It would be just like working at the office."

"Honey, I'm just getting ready to go to trial with a big case. I can't leave now."

"But I miss you, Dad. Mom would have wanted..." She caught herself. Guilting her dad into coming for a visit wasn't the answer, no matter how much she missed him. "I'm sorry. I didn't mean—"

"It's OK." He sighed, and then redirected. "Tell you what. As soon as this case is done, I'll take a break and come to see you. Give me a couple of weeks—a month, tops."

"Promise?"

"Yes. Of course."

"That would be great, Dad."

Carin removed the teabag from the cup as an awkward silence ensued. When her dad finally spoke, his voice was low—the voice he used when sharing important, confidential information with a client. "Carin, did you leave here because of Phillip...because of whatever happened there?"

"Please don't ask, Dad. I don't want to discuss it. Not now, at least. Maybe when you come to visit?"

"Can you wait that long, honey?"

"I...um..." She choked, sputtered, and bumped the cup so tea sloshed over the side to stain the counter. She quickly changed the subject. "I—I have to go now. I've got papers to grade and Hailey's waiting for me to call."

"Well...OK." She heard the catch in his voice, and it tore her heart just a bit. "I love you, sweetheart."

"I love you, too. Come soon, OK?" She pressed the end button and laid the phone on the counter. *Oh, how I wish Mama was still here. She'd listen and know what to do.* Why hadn't her mother shared what she sensed about Phillip? It would have made things so much easier in the long run.

She remembered Cameron's funeral, and it felt like a dream. Phillip was there, and he portrayed himself as the doting boyfriend, bringing her water, holding her hand. She'd felt comforted, felt like she had an ally as she struggled to keep her dad from collapsing under the stress of losing his only son so soon after losing his wife.

Then Phillip disappeared, and when she went to the parking lot for a gulp of fresh air—to ease the ache from her heart—she heard his voice carry on the breeze. He was laughing, mocking her voice, nasally with grief-filled tears. As she rounded the corner, she saw the raven-haired woman, too—an intern from her father's office.

The two were locked in an embrace, Phillip's cheek nuzzled in her dark hair. The words he spoke slashed like a knife. "I'll tell her I'm heading back to the office to finish up some work for her father. She'll never know the difference. Then I'll meet you at your place. Give me an hour."

The intern giggled as she slipped a hand beneath his suit jacket. "I'll be waiting..."

Carin eased back around the corner, caught between staying and fleeing. Phillip appeared suddenly, plowing into her, and bile leapt into her throat.

"In a hurry?" she asked.

"I...um..." It was a rare occurrence of speechlessness on his part. "I was coming to look for you."

"Oh, I'm sure you were." And she spun on her heel, marching back toward the building as tears blinded her. "Go to your *meeting*, Phillip. Your work here is finished."

She'd foolishly believed the pain that ripped through her at that very moment was the worst she'd ever feel. Little did she know the months to come would deal even more excruciating blows.

The grandfather clock in the living room chimed the hour, drawing Carin back. She reached for the delicate floral teacup from the set that used to belong to her mom and held the warm cup in both hands as she sipped chamomile tea. Her thoughts drifted to Jake...his easy smile and quick humor. Somehow, his gentle demeanor calmed the storm of doubts that swept through her. Could it be that God had brought them together for a purpose she had yet to fully understand?

# 7

"I don't know why I let you talk me into this," Carin grumbled as she helped Hailey move a landscape timber to the far side of the church playground. The earthy scent of mulch mixed with the crisp odor of pine needles that had fallen from bushes outside the playground fence. Maple leaves from trees in the side yard covered rich green grass in a blanket of gold and crimson. In the pasture beyond, rolled bales of hay dotted a horizon filled with smoke-hazed mountains. The air was mild and a slight breeze offset the heat of a warm early-October sun. "I have a stack of essays to grade and an evaluation first thing Monday morning."

"The papers can wait, and you'll do just fine on your evaluation. You're a great teacher, Carin. You'll earn a glowing review." Hailey dropped her end of the timber onto a pile and crossed the playground to haul another. They'd need at least two-dozen pieces of the heavy wood to box in the area around the jungle gym that a few of the men had just finished repairing. Then a healthy layer of mulch would be added to cushion any falls kids might take from the equipment. "Besides, you love the outdoors, and it's a beautiful day."

"I suppose."

"*And*"—Hailey winked and tilted her head toward the back doors of the church—"look who's coming this way."

Carin followed Hailey's gaze...*Jake*.

Her heart did a little two-step as he tugged a ball cap low over his eyes while he crossed the yard. His T-shirt clung to a terrain of muscles across his chest, and long, powerful legs were clad in faded blue jeans torn at one knee. He seemed much taller than she remembered, since she was wearing tennis shoes instead of her usual spiky sandals. As he neared, she inhaled clean soap and the scent of something purely masculine.

"Hello, Hailey...Carin." His gaze swept over her as he strode through the playground gate and pulled a pair of worn leather work gloves from the back pocket of his jeans. While he tugged them on, Carin remembered how she'd confused him for East Ridge Church's caretaker. Looking at his dark, shaggy hair tucked beneath the Tennessee Titans baseball cap and his scuffed work boots, it was easy to see why. "You're doing a great job whipping the playground into shape."

"We've barely put a dent in things." Carin smoothed wisps of hair that had escaped an elastic band she'd used to gather the curls into a tail. "There's still so much to do."

"All in good time." Jake reached for a box of long, oversized nails. "Would you two like to help me pound stakes into these timbers so we can form the box and lay some mulch?"

"Ahh...Carin will." Hailey backpedaled toward the fence as she ran a hand through spiky cinnamon hair. "I promised to help prepare lunch, and then I need to check on my kids in the nursery. Greg got called in to work at the fire hall last night, so I had to bring Noah and Zachary with me this morning. Anyway, I'll be heading...into the kitchen now."

"I see." The gleam in Jake's eyes said he understood her tactics all too well.

A school of jellyfish darted through Carin's belly as a splotch of heat crept up her neck. "In that case, will you put on an extra pot of coffee?"

"Sure. Consider it done."

As Hailey turned and scurried away, Carin's gaze swept the play area. Where were all the other volunteers, anyway? The grounds seemed suddenly deserted since the men had finished their repairs of the equipment and gone inside to work in the children's classrooms. Carin stood to brush dirt from the knees of her jeans. "Maybe I should help in the kitchen, too."

"No need. Mrs. Doran is in there heading up the team. And she has plenty of help."

"Well, I guess the work won't get done on its own." Carin forced down a sense of uneasiness and surveyed the pile of landscape timbers. The playground area would be much more aesthetic—not to mention much safer—as soon as they got the work finished. "Where's the hammer?"

"Here." Jake drew a large mallet from his tool belt. "How good is your aim?"

"That depends. How steady is your hold?"

Jake smirked. "I guess we'll find out."

"We'd better get started then." Carin reached for a handful of spikes. "This looks like as good a place as any."

Working together, they slipped the timbers into position. After a few poorly-aimed swings of the mallet, one that nearly crushed Jake's thumb, Carin conceded that Jake would do a better job hammering, so she held the spikes in place while he took aim with the mallet.

"So," Jake said between blows. "How's the journal writing going?"

"Corey's a natural." Carin gnawed her bottom lip as she lined up the oversized nail with a pre-drilled hole. "I must admit, he *has* provided quite a nice little window into your world."

"How so?" As Jake hammered, the box surrounding the play area took shape. He slipped another timber easily into place. "What do you mean?"

Carin laughed. "Well, I know your favorite candy is mini peanut butter cups, and you like to be early for everything, which drives Corey insane." She held tight as the timber shook while Jake hammered. "*And* you like corny vintage horror movies and have read every book ever written by Max Lucado—twice over."

"Corey wrote all that?"

"And more, but I can't divulge everything—teacher-student privilege, you know."

"Well, that's hardly fair." Jake sat back and wiped beads

of sweat from his brow with the hem of his T-shirt. "You know all kinds of things about me now, but I don't know anything about you—except for the green pens, of course."

Carin shrugged. "What more is there to know?"

"Let's see…" He rubbed the shadow of stubble across his chin. "How many years have you been teaching?"

"Six. I taught at a middle school in Nashville and then took a leave for two years while I helped out at my dad's law firm before I moved here." She'd helped her dad carry the workload when her mom had fallen ill…and then there had been Cameron to think about.

"Funny, you don't look battle weary from all the hours of slashing you must have put in."

She brushed hair from her brow. "If that was meant to be a compliment, you really need to work on your technique."

"Point taken."

Carin sat on the timber they'd just secured to catch her breath. Perspiration dampened the back of her neck, and she lifted her ponytail to fan herself with a free hand. "And just how many unsuspecting people have you duped into thinking you're the church caretaker?"

"I never said—"

"No, but you implied…"

"OK, guilty as charged." Jake pounded a nail as he spoke. "But it's my turn to ask the questions, so hold that thought."

"You've already met your quota of questions for the day." She drew a long, deep breath, stood, and reached for another timber. Dirt billowed around them and her arms ached as Jake rushed over to take it from her and dump it into place as if it was a match stick.

"So, I only get one question?" Jake lined up a second timber before he motioned to her for a spike. "That's pretty meager. I'd have to give you a D…if this was for a grade."

"OK." Giggles erupted as Carin swiped her soiled hands across the thighs of her jeans. "To be fair, I'll grant you two."

"Good." He positioned a spike and Carin held it firmly while he poised the mallet. "Then my second is…will you go to dinner with me?"

"What?" She bobbled the spike and Jake missed his mark. The mallet hit the edge of the timber and bounced from his hand to tumble into the dirt. "That's not...a valid question."

"Not valid..." He retrieved the mallet, brushed a layer of mud from the head, and gazed at her with confusion and a bit of mischief in his eyes. "It's a question, isn't it?"

She hunched her shoulders, a restless storm sweeping in to chill her. "I can't, Jake. I...shouldn't."

"Because you're Corey's teacher?"

"No."

"Because you're seeing someone?"

"*No.* Definitely no."

"Why, then? You don't like Chinese? We can go to McDonald's instead."

A shaky laugh escaped but quickly turned to frustration. Carin blew wisps of hair from her eyes. How could she share with him? He was a pastor...most likely perfect in every way. Even with Corey, he'd held his temper when most parents would have thrown in the towel. He stood before a congregation every Sunday, and she was a woman who hadn't stepped inside a church in nearly two years...except for last Sunday, and that didn't really count. What would he think of her if he knew her faith hung by the thinnest thread? She dipped her head and turned from him, shading her eyes. "You wouldn't understand."

"*I* wouldn't understand?" He stood and stretched the kinks from his back. His shoulders flexed beneath damp cotton fabric, revealing the definition of powerful muscles. "I'm a pastor, Carin. And, although this is a small church, believe me, I've heard it all."

"I..." Suddenly her voice caught and she removed her work gloves to swipe a hand across her eyes as they pooled with tears. She'd hardly slept the night before. The phone calls from Phillip, coupled with memories of her mom and Cameron, plagued her.

"Are you crying?" Jake swung around to face her full-on,

his expression startled.

"I...I've offended you." She turned away, mortified, and rubbed the damp palms of her hands across her weary eyes. "I didn't intend to. I'm sorry."

"Don't be sorry. It's OK." He peeled off his work gloves and took a bottle of water from the cooler propped near the fence. "Here, sit a minute and have something cold to drink."

"No, really. I'm fine." She reached for the spike that had toppled into the dirt when Jake missed his mark, and lined it up again. "Let's just finish this. It's nearly lunchtime."

Carefully, Jake took the spike from her. "The work can wait. Sit in the shade." He patted the landscape timber and pressed the cool bottle of water into her hands. "Talk to me."

"Oh, this is embarrassing." She shook her head, swiped her eyes once more, and uncapped the bottle to draw a sip of water. "Why would you want to go to dinner with someone who's so...mixed up?"

"We're all mixed up to some extent. You don't think I'm on a wild ride raising Corey? My life's filled with new adventures every day—some good, some not so good, and some just plain horrific."

"Jake, be real about this. You're a preacher and—"

His jaw clenched and his gaze pierced her. "I'm a man, too."

The realization sent a shiver up Carin's spine. She'd noticed...more than she ought to. She scooted across the timber, putting a bit of distance between them. "But I haven't been to church in years."

"You're here today."

"I didn't want to come. Hailey dragged me here because, well, she says I've lost my...belief, and I need my batteries recharged."

"Have you? Do you?"

Carin shrugged. "I guess. I mean...yes."

"Well, no matter what you think you've lost, faith hasn't lost you." Jake tapped her shoulder gently. "You have Him, Carin. You'll always have Him."

"Him? Who do you mean?"

Jake pointed heavenward, toward the cloudless blue sky. *"Him.* He'll never leave you, even if you get sidetracked and leave Him…for a while."

"How can you be so sure?"

"Trust. Faith. Hope. They're very powerful."

"I wish I could feel them." Carin's stomach churned, and she felt as if she was drifting aimlessly in a raging sea of doubt.

"You will. Trust me if you can't trust anything else right now. I promise…I've been where you are."

"You have?"

He reached for a second bottle of water and settled beside her in the shade of a maple tree that towered over the playground fence. The scent of him—strong and purely masculine—sent a tremor of longing through her. Carin was beginning to see him as a man, but would *he* see *her* as anything more than his brother's teacher…or a grieving woman…if she let him in? "You sound shocked. Are you surprised to learn the pastor's hit a few potholes in the road?"

"Maybe…yes."

"I'm not perfect…so I've learned to lean on Him. You can lean on Him, too. Whatever's riddling you with doubt, it's going to be OK. Maybe not easy, but OK."

"I…hope so."

"I *know* so." He drew a sip of water and leaned forward to murmur, "Carin, do you have a Bible?"

"No. I don't…I haven't…"

"We'll have to remedy that."

She could see in his gaze that the wheels were already turning.

"But for now, remember Deuteronomy 31:8, *'The Lord himself goes before you and will be with you; He will never leave you nor forsake you. Do not be afraid; do not be discouraged.'*"

"I like that." She mulled over the words. His voice soothed like balm, and she relaxed a bit. "Thank you, Jake." She wiped her eyes with a finger and drew a long, cleansing breath. "I feel so foolish for…this."

"Don't. Everyone gets down sometimes. Everyone doubts and flounders. It's OK. It's…human."

"Jake!" Corey's voice rang across the churchyard. "Lunch is ready."

Jake ignored the call and leaned over to Carin. "Better now?"

"Yes…a little, I guess." She trembled when his shoulder brushed hers.

He smiled. "A little is better than not at all, right?"

"Umm…uh-huh."

"Jake!"

Jake groaned and shook his head. "We'll be there in a minute," he called back. He sighed and stood, turning back to offer Carin a hand. "We'd better go before he wakes the babies in the nursery. Hailey would *not* be happy about that."

"Wait, Jake." Carin squeezed his hand. "For the record, I do…like Chinese food very much."

He squeezed back, grinning, and tugged her to her feet. "Friday night good for you, say six o'clock?"

"Perfect."

"*Jake!*"

"Ugh! Remind me to buy a gag for the kid." Jake tossed his work gloves beside the mallet and held onto Carin's hand as they started toward the church. "Yes, a gag would be good."

"I second that." Carin was surprised to find her tears had turned to laughter. The touch of his hand in hers gave her a little thrill—different than any she'd felt before.

Jake laughed, too, and paused to tuck a curl behind her ear. "Let's go see what Mrs. Doran has cooked up. I hope she baked some of her famous triple-chocolate, peanut butter fudge brownies. They're the best."

# 8

Carin felt pleased with the progress Corey was making at school. He was actually a huge help with the school newspaper, and the other students seemed to accept and respect him once she'd encouraged him to back off on his bossiness.

*And* she'd actually discovered him and Amy MacGregor laughing together as they edited a story about the upcoming book fair. Her intuition had paid off as far as the pair was concerned—Amy was coming out of her shell, and the chip on Corey's shoulder had shrunk a size or two. No more toy mice in her desk or spitballs on the white board, either—that was certainly an added bonus.

"You've worked hard enough today," Carin said as she watched the pair pore over the proof for the month's edition of the paper, which would go to print in the morning. "Clean things up and head home. You have a vocabulary test tomorrow, remember?"

"How could we forget?" Corey scribbled a few notes on the proof with the signature orange pen she'd provided. "I'm grounded again—for destroying Jake's cell phone. I didn't see it on the kitchen counter when I threw the football. Who knew it would end up in the dishwater? It was a perfect spiral, too, a real gun. Coach McCrosky would've been proud."

Carin stifled a grin as he mimed a slow-motion replay of the throw. "A pass like that might have scored the winning touchdown in the NFL," she agreed.

"Probably, but Jake didn't appreciate the effort like an NFL coach would have, so I might as well hang around here and work on this stuff. If I go home now, Jake will just put me to work mucking out the church bathrooms or something disgusting like that. He's pretty mad at me—again."

"Well…I guess you can work just a little bit longer." Carin gathered a stack of essays from her desk and tucked them into her tote. "Jake will be worried if you stay too much later, though."

"Tell me something I don't know." He shrugged. "But he'd probably be glad to get rid of me for a while, too. I try hard. Really I do, but I just can't seem to stay out of trouble."

"That's not true." Carin tossed a green pen into the tote then glanced up. "Corey, you don't *really* think Jake wants rid of you, do you?"

"No, I guess not. And I don't want him to worry, either." He sighed and shook shaggy bangs from his eyes. "I'll just stay a little bit longer. I promise."

"My mom's driving him home," Amy added. "We found out we only live a few blocks from each other. Isn't that cool?"

"Yes, very." Carin nodded and flipped open a steno book to check notes she'd jotted earlier. "I'm going to head down to the office to gather my messages and then be right back. You can work until I return, and Mrs. Carlisle's right next door if you need anything. Then it's quitting time. We'll finish the edits and go to print in the morning."

"Thanks, Miss O'Malley." Amy turned back to the computer screen.

"You're welcome."

Carin left the two with their heads bowed together, debating the correct spelling of a word. This was certainly a shift from Corey's refusal to work with Amy just a few weeks ago.

"I'll spell check it," Amy's voice drifted from the room, and Carin smiled to herself as she headed around the corner and toward the office. She met Hailey coming up the hall.

"Hey, you." Hailey greeted her in a voice raspy from fall allergies. She carried a colorful arrangement of autumn blooms and baby's breath in a delicate crystal vase tied with a silky sunshine-yellow bow. "How was your day?"

"Good. Who sent you those gorgeous flowers?" Carin gushed at the sweet floral scent.

"They're not for me." Hailey handed the vase to her. "They're for *you.*"

"Me? Who on earth are they from?"

Hailey tapped the card tucked into a small plastic holder. "I wanted to peek, but…"

Carin plucked the card from its holder and tore open the envelope.

"What does it say?" Hailey peered over her shoulder, and Carin felt warm breath tickle her neck. "Spill the beans."

Carin read aloud as she scanned the words. "Looking forward to tomorrow night. Jake."

"Jake? Pastor Jake?" Hailey's hazel eyes brightened. "Oh, Carin, that's wonderful! Why didn't you tell me?"

"What's to tell?"

"You're going out with him."

"Just to dinner. He's…simply a friend."

"Sounds like he wants to be more than a friend." Hailey winked conspiratorially. "And how about you? Do you want to be more than friends?"

"No…maybe…I don't know." Her insides bubbled with the idea. After lunch yesterday, she and Jake finished nailing the landscape timbers and helped unload and spread a truck's worth of mulch into the play area. When the work was done, they'd settled together beneath the shade of the pavilion, sharing a plate of chocolate chip cookies and more bottled water. His laid-back attitude and quick humor put her at ease, and she didn't remember laughing so hard—enjoying the day so thoroughly—since…well…forever. "I haven't thought much about it. It's…confusing."

"So, maybe you want to be more than friends, right? And maybe is good." Hailey nodded approval. "Maybe has potential. Greg and I started out with a maybe, and look where we are now."

"Happily married with two kids and a dog."

Hailey leaned in and splayed a hand over her belly. "And

another on the way—a kid, that is. Not a dog."

"No!" Carin gasped with pleasure. "Really?"

"Yes. I just found out yesterday, and you're the first one I've told, besides Greg, of course."

"Oh, Hailey, that's wonderful news!" Carin jostled the arrangement into one arm and hugged Hailey with her other. "Three beautiful kids. Wow. I'm so happy for you."

"Thanks. But enough about me." She handed Carin a small package wrapped in a baby-blue lace bow. "This came with the flowers, too."

A slight thrill danced up Carin's spine. She handed the arrangement to Hailey and turned the package over in her hands. "What do you think it is?"

"Feels like a book of some sort. I don't know. Open it!"

Carin tore eagerly at the wrapping to find Hailey's guess was spot-on. Inside she found a small Bible. It was scuffed and worn, and when she opened the navy front cover a note slipped out. She caught the paper before it fluttered to the polished tile floor.

*Dear Carin,*

*This book has traveled many miles and seen me through more challenging times than I can number. It's guided me well, and now I'd like you to have it.*

*Jake*

"Wow." Hailey dabbed her nose with a tissue. "Look at that."

Carin flipped through the Bible pages, many dog-eared, and saw that several passages were highlighted and a few marked with colorful neon strips of post-it notes. "It's...really too much."

"No, it's not, Carin. It's just right." Hailey handed the flowers over. "How did you meet Jake, anyway?"

"Remember how you suggested I talk to him about Corey? Well, I went over to the church that afternoon and he was mowing. Except I didn't know it was him, and..." She sighed, shaking her head.

"Long story, huh?"

"Exactly."

"The good ones always are. Looks like you've got some reading to do."

Carin slipped a finger across the worn leather. "Yes, I guess I do."

"Better get going, then. I'll herd Corey and Amy from your room, get them moving on home. You go on."

"Thanks, Hailey."

"Don't mention it."

Carin's belly flip-flopped as she strode through the school's front door and into cool afternoon sunshine. She breathed in the sweet scent of flowers while she balanced the vase on the passenger seat and wedged it into place with her filled tote bag. Then she leaned against the car and gathered her cell phone. A quick call to information connected her directly to the number she needed. It was late, and the church secretary had probably left an hour ago, but maybe she'd still catch Jake.

"East Ridge Church." Jake answered on the second ring. "May I help you?"

Carin could barely contain her laughter. "I hear you mow lawns, and I'm looking for a caretaker to tame my grass."

A slight hesitation, then, "Carin, is that you?"

She burst into laughter. "Yes, Jake, it's me."

"Well, this is a nice surprise."

"Talk about surprises—I called to thank you for the flowers...and the Bible. The floral arrangement is lovely, and the Bible—well, are you sure you want to part with it?"

"I already have. I want you to have it."

Carin warmed at the sincerity in his tone. "Thank you." She lowered her voice and turned her face to the sunshine. "I'm looking forward to tomorrow night, too."

"Oh, about tomorrow..." Jake paused and she heard him tap a pencil on the desk blotter that kept track of his appointments. "I have a small problem."

"You do?" For a fleeting moment she thought maybe he'd found out—somehow, some way—about what had happened with Cameron…and maybe Phillip, too.

"Yes," Jake continued. "You see, I don't have any idea where you live."

*Relief.* "Oh, that. Well, that's a problem I'll be more than happy to help you solve." She gave him her address.

"Thanks. Problem solved. Now, if they were only *all* that easy."

"Um, Jake?" Carin cradled the phone between her ear and shoulder and leaned toward the passenger window. A gust of wind carried the musty scent of leaves and the cool nip of fall.

"Yes?"

"Corey's just leaving school. He and Amy have been working on the school paper. He told me about getting grounded for ruining your cell phone. He also said if he comes home too early you'll make him—and I quote—muck out the church bathrooms tonight."

"Muck out…oh, brother. I think you should have recruited him for the drama club instead of the newspaper staff."

"Not a bad idea." Carin laughed again. "Anyway, I just thought you'd want to know in case he's a bit late. Amy's mom is driving him home."

"Yeah, he told me that this morning. Can you believe it, after how hard he fought not to work with her? I think the two are becoming an item."

"Ironic, I know."

"I appreciate all you're doing to help him. It's been a rough road."

"I can only imagine." She thought about Cameron, wished for the millionth time she might have helped him, too. "Maybe you'd like to share…sometime."

"I would. Anyway, I think I'll meet Corey at the door with a mop and a bucket just to see his reaction."

"Now, *that* I'd like to watch."

"Tune in for tonight's journal-writing. Should be interesting." Jake paused and lowered his voice. "See you tomorrow night?"

Carin's heart leapt at the thought. "Yes. I'll be waiting."

❧❦

Jake arrived a bit early to pick up Carin, so he took his time strolling up the walk to her tidy house. The white, clapboard siding was surrounded by a planked-wood porch. Hardy mums grew tall and full in the front flower beds, adding waves of yellow and crimson. Maple trees shed orange and gold leaves that danced across the grass like confetti. He breathed in their rich, musty scent and was glad for sunshine that staved off the chill of a slight autumn breeze.

Carin surprised him by opening the door just as he was about to knock. The sight of her in a knee-length, flowing skirt paired with a floral blouse stopped him in his tracks. Her hair was pulled back, twisted and secured with a delicate silver clip, showing off the sleek curve of her neck and striking, emerald eyes. The warm scent of sandalwood clung to her skin.

"Wow."

"Wow, what?" Her eyebrows knit together.

"You look...wow."

"You clean up pretty good yourself." Her gaze swept the length of him. She nodded appreciatively then stepped back from the doorway. "C'mon in." She ushered him into a cozy living room. Plump burgundy pillows decorated a tan couch, and a dog-eared paperback lay open on the side table. The scent of cinnamon wafted from a candle on the coffee table. Carin bent to extinguish the flame. "I'm almost ready. I just have to feed Scooter."

"Scooter?"

"My cat." A gray ball of fur bolted through the doorway and skidded across the hardwood floor to wrap itself around Jake's ankles. "His name's Scooter."

"Hey, Scooter." Jake knelt to scratch between the cat's spiked ears, and he purred like a semi roaring down the highway.

"He likes you." Carin nodded. "That's a good sign.

Animals have good instincts about people."

"Whew." He swiped a hand across his brow. "I'm glad I passed that test."

"Me, too. If he'd tried to bite you, I would have had to send you packing."

"So he's, like, your dating barometer, huh?" Jake laughed and scooped the cat into his arms. "Hey, buddy, meet your new best friend. We need to have a long talk, OK?"

Carin laughed as he purred and burrowed against Jake's chest. "Just let me put some food in his bowl, and we can go."

Jake followed her into the kitchen with the cat in his arms. Waning sunlight danced through the window over the sink, bathing cheery-white cabinets. The flowers he'd sent graced the center of a polished dinette table, and their sweet scent filled the room. The Bible lay open at a chair, a half-drained glass of iced tea beside it.

"I was reading," Carin explained as she followed his gaze.

Jake set Scooter down and pressed a finger to the Bible. "Do you mind?"

"No. Go right ahead." Carin reached into the cabinet to the left of the sink for a can of cat food. She spooned the tuna mixture into Scooter's dish that was set out on a plastic mat near French doors that opened onto a small patio. The cat brushed against her legs and cranked his motor up a notch.

Jake picked up the Bible and grazed his fingers over the passage he'd highlighted five years earlier, when he'd decided to leave his job as a CPA at Carson and Brewer to become a pastor. It had been a confusing time, because the wordly part of him was attached to all the toys and gadgets the money brought in, while his heart longed for something more—much more. His dad had understood, and they'd talked through the confusion until Jake had found the path he was meant to travel. But now his dad was gone. Jake cleared his throat and brushed a dark cloud of sadness aside. "Ah, Proverbs. And one of my favorite verses, too."

"What's that?"

*"'Trust in the Lord with all your heart and lean not on your*

*own understanding. But in all your ways acknowledge Him and He shall guide your path.'"*

"Hmm...yes. I love that one, too. But it's a hard one to accept."

"Why?"

"Because sometimes things happen...and they don't make sense at all."

"Like...?"

Carin sighed. "Like my friend Lilly. She has the onset of Alzheimer's, and she gets confused sometimes. She's all alone now, in a room at the senior center, except for when I go to visit her. And sometimes she doesn't even know who I am, and it breaks my heart, so..."

"So, that *was* you." Jake shook his head. "I thought so."

"What are you talking about?"

"I saw you at the center last Thursday evening after I came to visit you at school. You were coming back from the pond, pushing a woman in a wheelchair."

"That was Lilly." She shifted feet. "I'm sorry. I didn't see you, Jake."

"I hurried to get out there with Pastor Julian, but you were already gone."

"Lilly likes the pond. She thinks she sees her late husband there."

"Pastor Julian says the same thing...about his wife."

"Do you think there's something to it?"

"Why not? They believe there is." Jake shrugged. "Pastor Julian swears he smells the spearmint his wife used to grow in their backyard garden. And the funny thing is, lately I smell it, too."

Carin gasped. "Lilly grows spearmint in a small box she keeps near her window."

"Where's her room?"

"First hall to the right, next to the last room on the left."

"Well, that explains the spearmint, at least." Jake rubbed his chin and smiled. "Pastor Julian just moved in next door to her."

# 9

"Ming Tree Restaurant." Carin scanned the vibrant black and red marquee as Jake made a right turn off the main road. "I've never heard of it."

"No?" Jake maneuvered the Jeep into a parking space and killed the engine. "Then you're in for a real treat. You're about to sample the best Chinese food in the state."

"Money back guarantee, huh?"

"In full." Jake slipped from the driver's side and came around to open the door for her. Cool evening air caused ripples to dance across the surface of the river beyond. A few strands of Carin's hair escaped from a silver clip, caressing smooth, flushed cheeks. A gentle breeze carried the scent of her perfume. She pulled a cotton sweater over her shoulders.

"It's pretty here."

"Yes, especially on a clear evening like this, when the sun dips below the horizon." He watched her tilt her face into the breeze and breathe in the scent of autumn leaves that rustled along the riverbank. "After dinner we can take a walk along the river boulevard, if you'd like."

"That sounds nice. I would like to...very much."

He followed her up the walk and through double wooden doors decorated in an Asian motif. The soft melody of a mandolin wafted from the foyer, and a lighted saltwater aquarium boasted giant koi fish that swam in a slow, mesmerizing cadence. The fish reminded Jake of Corey, who always liked to pause for a moment to make silly faces through the aquarium glass. He hoped Corey wasn't giving Patrick and Julie too much trouble.

The aroma of marinated meats and vegetables filled the

air. Jake's stomach growled as an older, portly Chinese woman named Sulee greeted them.

"Hello, Pastor Jake." A broad smile revealed a slight gap between her two front teeth. Her dark hair, peppered with gray, was smoothed into a tight, neat bun. She wiped her hands on a starched white apron. "And who's this?"

"Sulee, I'd like you to meet Carin O'Malley."

"Well, hello there. Nice to meet you, Miss O'Malley. Welcome." Her head bobbed as she reached for Carin's hand. "I have a special table reserved for you."

The aroma of won-ton soup and egg rolls washed over Jake as Sulee led them through the restaurant, past booths tucked into corners and tables bathed in the soft glow of light from paper lanterns, to a wall of windows. There she motioned to a table with a river view backdropped by cloud-haloed Smoky Mountains.

"Oh, Jake, it's wonderful." Carin gazed out the expanse of windows as waning sunlight masked in hues of frothy peach and ripe berry danced across the horizon. "What an amazing sunset."

"Thanks, Sulee." Jake winked. "This is perfect."

She handed them menus. "Would you like the usual, or do you need a few minutes?"

"The usual?" Carin asked.

"Beef and broccoli," Jake tapped the menu. "Gotta have my greens."

"That sounds good." Carin nodded. "I'll have the same."

Sulee nodded. "Perfect choice." She smiled at Carin and poured steaming Chinese tea into a gold-rimmed, floral teacup. "Jake, you have a very pretty girl with you today. Smart, too. Left Corey at home, yes?"

"He's with a friend. You remember Dillon?"

"Of course—the boy who spilled soda all over the floor and broke two glasses playing table hockey with a wadded piece of paper?"

"Ouch." Jake grimaced. "Yes, that's Dillon."

"I remember." She nodded again. "Good for you to have

some quiet time to share dinner with such a nice girl. Enjoy…both of you."

"Table hockey?" Carin grinned as Sulee turned to leave, murmuring fervently in Chinese. "Come here often?"

"More than I should. Corey likes the food, and Sulee always gives him a handful of fortune cookies filled with Bible verses and unique messages. He gets a kick out of cracking each one open to read."

"Yes, I think he did mention something about fortune cookies in his journal."

Jake laughed. "What has he *not* mentioned in his journal?"

Carin sipped her tea and a cloud of steam billowed over the rim of the cup. "He hasn't written anything about your parents. Not a word."

"Still too raw, I expect." Jake reached for the tea.

"What happened, Jake, to your parents?"

Jake leaned back in the chair and sighed as her question brought on an onslaught of memories. Even now, nearly a year later, the answer came with great difficulty. "Corey was at a church retreat when he got real sick—ruptured appendix. My mom and dad were rushing to get to the hospital, because the doctors hurried him into surgery. It was raining, and they were on I-40 at the state line into North Carolina, passing a semi when one of its tires blew. The car flipped into a culvert and they both…died instantly." The news had come on a storm-laden Saturday evening, and in his mind Jake heard the echo of wiper blades as he raced down the highway to get to Corey before he came out of surgery. The memory was surreal, even now, right down to the song that played on the radio as he pulled into the hospital parking lot and found a police officer waiting in the emergency room.

"Oh." Carin leaned in, her voice high and tight. "That's a dangerous stretch of highway on a good day. I'm so sorry, Jake."

"Corey took it really hard. He was close to Mom, but even more so to Dad. I'd been out of the house for a long time, and I've felt the loss for sure, but not like Corey. He was just...devastated. He went through a rough time, Carin. A really rough time."

"But he's coming through it...and you, too?"

"I'm not going to sugarcoat it. Having Corey come to live with me was like having a bomb dropped in my lap. Total upheaval, loads of chaos. And the emotional trauma he's endured, it's been nearly insurmountable. That's why I appreciate so much...how you're helping him. He's on the right path now. He's a smart kid, and he's got a lot of people pulling for him. He'll figure things out." Jake sighed. "Anyway, I've done some real soul searching. Why did this happen? Why has Corey had to suffer so much? But through it all, believe it or not, my faith has grown stronger. God has me where He wants me."

"You sound so sure. I wish I could be sure, too." Her gaze locked with his. "You're a very strong person, Jake."

"I don't know." He shook his head. "Some days I don't think so, but I pray a lot and somehow manage to put one foot in front of the other. I know God has a plan, and I cling to that. Having the responsibility of raising Corey, well, it's humbled me tremendously. I used to be what you might call a know-it-all. But now I'm convinced that all I know could fit into the barrel of one of those green pens you like so much."

"'I can do all things through Christ who strengthens me,'" Carin quoted. "You highlighted that verse in the Bible you gave me."

"I did, didn't I?" He remembered the moment he'd done so as clearly as if it were today, and it gave his gut a jolt.

"I suppose it holds some special significance for you."

"Yes, it does."

"How? Why?"

"Because at the time I was covered in grief...drowning in it. My folks had just died, and Corey was still in the hospital recovering from his surgery. He kept asking for our mom...and for Dad. So, finally, I had to tell him what had happened." He sighed, and in Carin's gaze he saw the depths of his own grief. "It's the hardest thing I've ever done."

"I can't begin to...imagine."

"Patrick spent a lot of time with me at the hospital. Neither of my folks had any siblings and all my grandparents are gone, so it's just...Corey and me." He drew a long sip of soda and remembered how Corey had sobbed for nearly two straight days, until the exhaustion of his own grief, coupled with the help of some powerful sedatives, sent him into a deep, dreamless sleep. "I don't know what I would have done without Patrick and Julie, too. They've been like a lifeline."

"Corey has mentioned them a lot in his journal. They seem like very caring people."

"Oh, that doesn't begin to put a dent in it. Patrick carried the load at church until I got back on my feet. And Julie, well, she took Corey under her wing, got him and Dillon buddied up. Those two are mischief together, for sure, but I wouldn't have it any other way."

"And you...?" Carin's gaze was filled with questions. "Has anyone taken you under their wing?"

Jake thought of Rachelle and the way she'd balked at the idea of him taking custody of Corey. Her voice echoed through his head like an annoying refrain.

*You really want to sacrifice the next seven years of your life— our lives—for a kid who's not even your own?*

He'd tried his best to reason with her, to make her understand his need to protect Corey, to nurture him. Their brother-bond was rock-solid strong, despite their age difference. But in the end, Rachelle refused to budge.

"It's him or me, Jake." She'd crossed her arms and turned her back to him, her dark eyes like two cold stones, and he knew without a second thought what road he would take. "Choose carefully," she'd added, and the chilling words coupled with a defiant tilt of her chin only served to cement Jake's decision.

Even now, the callous words and cold gleam that sharpened her gaze made Jake seethe. How could he have been so foolish to fall in love with someone so selfish and shallow? How could he not see? The depth of his blindness shamed him as he remembered the way she'd tossed her engagement ring onto the kitchen table, as if it held no value—no meaning—at all. The echo as it bounced over the Formica surface matched the staccato gunshot of her high heels across the polished wood floor as she stormed out the front door of his house.

Jake trained his eyes on Carin and forced the memory away. "I lean on God," he said. But he knew from the look in Carin's eyes that *she* knew...the human side of him, the man, needed more, longed for more. The road was long and lonely and filled with detours that would be so much easier to navigate...with the help of another. He swallowed hard and prayed for a change of subject. Just then, Sulee rounded the corner. Jake leaned forward. "Look, here comes our food."

Sulee set the plates on the table and steam from fried rice billowed up like a cloud. "I made it extra special, just for you." She grinned her gap-toothed smile and nodded in a short, quick burst. "Enjoy."

Jake drew a breath. *Be completely humble and gentle; be patient, bearing with one another in love.* Ephesians 4:2 washed over him, and he felt a quiet strength restore his mood. What good would his resentment about events from the past serve now? *I need to look forward, not back.*

He cleared his throat. "Do you mind if I say grace?"

"Please...do." Carin bowed her head as Jake reached for her hand. Her skin was warm and smooth against his callused palms, and as his fingers brushed her wrist she twitched. He felt her pulse quicken to a cadence that mirrored his.

"Dear Lord, bless this food, and thank you for this time together. May we remember to trust in You and stay strong in You. For You, God, are the true Rock, our fortress and anchor in the many storms of life. Amen."

"Amen," Carin echoed.

He was glad the prayer didn't seem to make her uncomfortable. Maybe giving her the Bible had helped. He knew from experience that just because someone abandoned the church, it didn't mean their faith was abandoned, as well.

Jake was reluctant to let go of the delicate fingers that had twined with his. But somehow he managed and reached for his fork. "Dig in."

"Mmm, it smells delicious." Carin speared a broccoli sprig slathered in a rich, dark sauce. "How's yours?"

"Perfect." Jake chewed, swallowed, and scooped another bite. "Corey usually orders the Eight Treasure Chicken, but this…it's my staple food."

"When's the next work day at church?" Carin asked, dabbing the corner of her mouth with a cloth napkin.

"Are you thinking of dropping by to help again?" Jake drew a sip of tea.

"Maybe."

"I can use a hand with the memory garden tomorrow around nine o'clock. I'm going to pressure wash the engraved memorial bricks and re-lay them more evenly. Over time they've sunk into the ground quite a bit, and weeds have taken over."

"I might be able to carve out an hour or two to help and still get all my slashing done." Carin's eyes smiled over the rim of her glass as she sipped tea.

Jake laughed. "Wear something warm. Corey and Dillon will be there to help, too, and if they get ahold of the pressure washer, you're bound to get drenched."

"I can hold my own, but your advice is duly noted."

Sulee approached the table carrying a small plate with two fortune cookies. "Time for dessert," she said as she set the plate between Jake and Carin.

Carin handed one cookie to Jake and took the second.

"Wait. We have to open them at the same time," Jake said as she began to peel away the plastic wrap.

"What? Why?"

"It's tradition. Now count to three and crack yours open. One, two, three!"

The delicate cookies snapped and slips of paper fluttered onto the table.

"Read yours," Jake urged.

Carin picked up her slip and scanned the words. "On one side it reads, *'The Lord is good, a refuge in times of trouble. He cares for those who trust in Him.'* Nahum 1:7. And the other side says, 'God will give you the desires of your heart.'"

"No way." Jake studied his own fortune with disbelief. "It can't be…"

"Why? What does yours say?"

"It says, 'God will give you the desires of your heart.'" He flipped the slip over. "And—"

"Let me see." Carin took the paper. "'*The Lord is good, a refuge in times of trouble. He cares for those who trust in Him.'*"

They exchanged slips of paper to give the words a second look and sure enough, both of them had the very same fortune.

"What are the chances?" Carin whispered.

"I've been here a hundred times, and Corey and I have never, ever…"

Sulee ambled back to the table. "You get good messages?" She leaned to peer over Jake's shoulder.

"They're both exactly the same."

"Let me see those." She took both slips of paper, studied them, and the gap-toothed smile traveled from her lips to her eyes. "This is a very good thing. It's God's plan. Good things are in store for you—both of you. You see, just wait." Sulee waggled a finger at Jake. "It's about time you found a nice girl to share God's message with, Pastor Jake. Good man like you…God smiles on that. Mark my words. You'll see."

☙◦❧

"I'll bet Scooter's wondering where you've been," Jake said as they eased up the drive to Carin's house. "I might not be on his good side anymore, keeping you out so late."

"It *is* late." She glanced at her delicate silver watch. "But I had a good time. Walking along the river, sitting in one of the swings and watching the stars dance over the water for a while, was…nice."

"Yes, it was." Jake parked beneath a maple tree and killed the engine. Night sounds whispered around them and leaves rustled across the grass in the breeze. Moonlight cast a glow inside the truck, outlining Carin like a shadow. Jake longed to draw her close and kiss her. He cleared his throat. "I'll walk you to the door."

"Yeah." Carin gathered her purse and slipped the long, thin strap over one shoulder. "I forgot to leave a light on, so that would be next on the agenda."

"It would be next on the agenda, anyway." Jake eased from the driver's side and rounded the front of the Jeep to open the passenger door for her. "Do you think Scooter would mind if we did this again?"

"I think Scooter would be OK with it." Carin tugged her sweater across her shoulders to ward off the night chill. "What about Corey?"

"I'm sure he'll be completely and utterly mortified, but he'll get over it—eventually." Jake laughed as they made their way slowly up the walk. "Besides, it's nice payback. He's certainly put me in my own fair share of embarrassing situations."

"Duly documented and journaled." Carin grinned and nodded. "OK, I'll be your accomplice. Thank you, Jake."

"For what?"

She turned to face him as they reached the door. "For such a good time."

"Really?"

She dipped her head, sighing, and her gaze locked with his. "Definitely."

He brushed a knuckle across her cheek, felt her shiver. "Then I don't think I can let it end…without asking you."

Her breath was warm on his neck. "Asking me what?"

"If I can kiss you." His gaze captured hers. "I think I'd lie awake all night wondering about it."

Her emerald eyes fluttered delicately. "And if you *do* kiss me?"

"I'll lie awake all night thinking about *that*, too."

She took his hand, twined her fingers with his. "Well, in that case…"

He leaned into her, brushed his lips against hers, breathing in the scent of her. Her touch, a gentle caress of her palm against his cheek, ignited a flash of heat that raced up his spine.

"Hmm…I felt something…" Carin murmured and pressed a hand to her chest. "Right here."

"Maybe I'd better kiss you again, so you can be sure."

"Maybe…"

Jake gathered her into his arms and kissed her once more. When he finally stepped back, the stars seemed like flames ignited across the sky.

"Anything that time?" He stroked a wave of hair from Carin's eyes.

"Yes…definitely." She nodded and caught her lower lip between her teeth. "And you?"

"Uh-huh." He tucked a curl behind her ear and skimmed her cheek. "Now I know."

"Know what?"

"That I'll lie awake all night, for sure…thinking about this, about you."

"Me, too."

Jake took her house key and unlocked the door for her. "Can I pick you up tomorrow…to help with the memory garden?"

"Nine o'clock, you said?"

"Sounds about right."

"I'd like that. Yes."

"OK, then." He waited while she turned on the living room lights, and then did a quick sweep of the room for good measure. "Good night, Carin. I'll see you in the morning."

# 10

"I think we've managed to tame the weeds," Jake said as he tossed the last bunch of tangled roots into the trash. "Would you like to take a break before we start on the bricks?"

"No." Carin shook her head as she lifted one of the bricks from the dirt. "Look at them, Jake, all lopsided and muddied. It just seems...disrespectful. We have to fix them."

Jake was deeply touched by her concern and thought of the way Rachelle had balked at the idea of getting her hands soiled when he suggested they work together in the garden last spring. It wasn't right to compare, he chastised himself. The past was best left in the past. Yet he couldn't seem to help himself.

"Oh, Jake. This one belongs to your parents." Carin smoothed a hand over the mud-caked surface. "Ken and Susan...such proud names. They must have been wonderful people."

Jake's throat tightened. "Yes, they were," he managed.

"You must miss them terribly."

"I do."

"Let's begin here, OK?" Without waiting for his consent, Carin tugged the marble brick until it loosened from the ground. One by one, she lifted the row of bricks that arced in a semi-circle around the edge of the garden. She and Jake worked together, smoothing the dirt beneath and adding a layer of paving sand to level the area before carefully replacing each brick and gently washing it with a pressure-washer set on the gentlest flow.

"We used to have a group that maintained the gardens on the church grounds," Jake explained as he moved on to the next row of bricks. "Mrs. Staley headed it up. But when she died last fall, things sort of disintegrated. It's embarrassing, really, that the garden fell into such disrepair."

"You can't do it all, Jake." Carin dipped a cup into the bag of paving sand and scooped up enough to level the next few bricks. She smoothed the sand over the ground, and then backed away a bit to allow Jake room to reset the row. "Your plate's already overflowing. I like to garden. I wouldn't mind to help. And I'll ask Hailey to see if she can coax some of the other women into helping, too. Or maybe her Sunday school class...kids always like to help with stuff like this."

"Really? That would be great."

"Yes. I mean...if you'd like me to."

"Of course I'd like that."

"Is it too late to have a few bricks engraved and placed here among the others?"

"For whom?"

"For my mom. She died two years ago." Carin hesitated, and a cloak of sadness dimmed the glow of her emerald eyes. "And...for my brother, Cameron. He died last May."

"Your mom *and* your brother?" Jake shoved the bag of paving sand aside and sat on the sidewalk, crossing his legs. He eased her down beside him. "I had no idea. I'm so sorry, Carin. What happened?"

"My mom had ovarian cancer. By the time the doctors found it, the tumors raged through her like wildfire. She gave it a good fight anyway, but she couldn't...it wouldn't..."

Carin smoothed a hand over the row of bricks as tears filled her eyes, and Jake felt her grief as if it was his own.

"It's OK." He brushed a smudge of dirt from her forehead. "Let it out, Carin. It's not good to hold the hurt inside."

"So much pain...such unnecessary loss." Carin wiped her eyes with the sleeve of her flannel shirt. "I miss her every day. I miss Cameron, too."

"How old was he?"

"Just seventeen. He died...two days after he turned

seventeen."

"We can have a brick engraved for your mom," Jake assured her, "and for Cameron, too. Write down what you want each to say, and I'll take care of the rest, OK?"

Carin nodded and smiled through her tears. Wet streaks that ran down her cheeks glinted in the sunlight and left a trail through flecks of dirt that clung to her skin. "Thank you, Jake."

"You're welcome." He removed his work gloves and offered her a hand. "We're done here, for now. Would you like to take a drive with me? I have something I want to show you."

"What about Corey?"

"He's got a guitar lesson with Julie in half an hour. He and Dillon can finish up their work in the front yard until then, and then Patrick and Julie invited Corey over for the afternoon. The boys still have some work to do on that science project."

"The one with the ant farm?"

"Yeah. And apparently, one of the boys forgot to secure the cover after their last observation, so the colony relocated to Julie's pantry and got into the dog food. The two will be starting over—after they clean up the mess."

"Never a dull moment with those two, right?" Carin tugged off her gloves and wiped the tears from her cheeks with the palm of her hand.

"You said it."

☙❧

Carin's hair danced in a breeze that rushed through the passenger window of Jake's Jeep. Soft music filtered from the radio as he steered south through traffic. He'd tugged a ball cap low over his brow and rolled the sleeves of his flannel work shirt so she saw the taut muscles of his forearms and the strength of his hands. That strength didn't incite fear in her the way Phillip's strength tended to when his temper flared.

Instead, Carin felt a longing to know Jake better, to peel back the layers and find the man.

She remembered the kiss—two kisses, actually—that they'd shared last evening. Her lips still tingled from Jake's touch, and though she knew it was best to keep her distance, she yearned for more.

"I love it out here," Jake murmured as the traffic thinned and the Smoky Mountains soared majestically into an expanse of blue sky. "I never get tired of looking at the mountains, of seeing the burst of color that autumn brings."

"It's beautiful." Carin inhaled the musty scent of leaves that changed color before her eyes. A cool breeze kissed her cheeks. "Do you smell the wild onions?"

"Yes…the last hint of summer before full-blown autumn kicks in."

Jake rounded a curve and the road suddenly forked sharply. He swung the wheel to the right, and the Jeep scaled a winding gravel drive that ended abruptly in a grassy knoll.

"Walk with me?" He asked as he parked the Jeep. He grabbed a faded patchwork quilt from the backseat and gathered it into his arm as he hopped onto the grass and strode around the front of the Jeep to open her door. "I want to show you something."

"OK." Carin slid from the passenger seat, and Jake slipped his hand into hers. "I like it here. It's…more than beautiful."

"I think so, too."

Together they made their way across the grass to where a massive oak tree stood sentinel. Its trunk spanned at least five feet in diameter, and the breadth of its branches formed a shady canopy over the knoll. The scent of its fallen leaves reminded Carin of the warm pumpkin-spice bread her mom always made for Thanksgiving, and she smiled at the memory.

"Oh, Jake. This tree is…" She struggled for a word that might do it justice, came up blank and had to settle for, "amazing…wonderful." She stroked the rough bark and then hugged the tree, attempting to span the trunk with her arms until the futility made her laugh. "How old do you suppose it is?"

Jake pressed his hand to the back of hers and together they ran their fingers along the coarse trunk. "My guess is a couple hundred years, at least."

"Wow." Carin craned her neck to gaze through the branches into the cerulean sky. "That's pretty old. I don't think I've ever seen a tree this old."

"I'd say it can tell a story or two," Jake murmured, his breath warm against her cheek. Through the fabric of her cotton T-shirt, she felt the tautness of his chest muscles pressed to her back. "I call it my wisdom tree."

"Your wisdom tree?" Carin turned to face him and the blue of his eyes, the strength of his stance, filled her with a sudden wave of longing. "W-why?"

"Come over here and sit with me, and you'll see." Jake left her long enough to spread the quilt along the base of the trunk, then coaxed her beside him with a pat of his hand against the carefully-stitched cotton squares. She settled in beside him, leaning her back against the trunk and stretching her legs over the quilt's soft fabric. "Look out there." Jake motioned with his hand.

Carin followed his gaze and her breath caught. The view of the valley below, backdropped by a crisp canvas of cloud-veiled mountains, was like a beautiful watercolor painting, expertly brush-stroked.

"Oh, my..." She couldn't speak for the lump that crowded her throat. "It's... breathtaking." The sun formed a halo of light over the mountains, like a jeweled crown. And the mountains...they were a palette of maroon, earthy taupe and orange sherbet swirled together with the deepest blue-green. Carin felt as if she could reach out and touch their rounded tops.

"I know." Jake sighed and took her hand. His gaze fell over the mountains, and she thought she saw a flicker of something...regret, maybe. Or perhaps he simply wished for simpler, less hectic times. It couldn't be easy by any stretch of the imagination—the kinds of things he dealt with on a daily basis. Carin twined her fingers with his. "I come up here to sit when life gets all jumbled," he continued. "It helps me to let go of the worry, and to remember how small I am and how great God's power is."

"So that's why you gave it the name—"

"Yeah." He nodded to emphasize. "My wisdom tree."

"Oh, Jake, whose land is this?"

"It belonged to my grandparents and then my parents. And now it's been passed down to me."

"It's so amazing." Carin couldn't draw her gaze away. "I could sit here all day, just taking in the view, the scents...the soothing brush of the breeze through the leaves."

"God made all this." Jake's hand swept across the mountains. "Everything you see, He made just for us. How can anyone doubt His love...or His plan?"

Carin sighed, remembering the night of Cameron's funeral, so soon after her mom's...and the way Phillip had mocked her grief. Angry, overwhelmed by resentment, she'd turned her back on God.

"I...I'm embarrassed to say I've doubted, Jake." She twisted a curl around her index finger. "Things have happened...things I'm not proud of."

"You can trust me, Carin."

*You can trust me...*the threatening echo of Phillip's voice gave her chills. He'd taken her trust and shattered it. Could she really trust anyone—ever again?

Jake seemed to sense her unease. "If you can't trust me— yet, then trust God. He brought you here for a reason. He knows what He's doing."

"Maybe, but—" Carin sat up suddenly and pointed across the valley below. "Look, Jake. Is that the senior center? I think I see the pond."

"It is." Jake nodded. "You have eagle eyes, Carin."

"The water sparkles beneath the sunlight like a precious jewel."

"It always seems to sparkle, even when clouds cover the

sky." Jake leaned in, brushed the pad of his thumb across her cheek. "Maybe it does have some healing powers...at least as far as it seems to calm Pastor Julian when he's near it."

"Lilly always seems more aware, less restless, when she's near the water, too."

"I have to admit, I find a bit of serenity there, too." Jake leaned back against the trunk and sighed. "The pond...my wisdom tree...there's not a care in the world when you look at things from here."

"Why didn't your grandparents or your parents build a house here?" Carin asked. "They must have loved it as much as you do."

"I'm not sure. My dad always said that my grandparents bought it as an investment, and my grandfather used to pitch a chair up here and just get lost in the sights and smells. I don't think he ever had any intention of building—he simply liked to look. And my parents planned to construct their dream house when my dad retired from his job as an architect. But they never got the chance."

"And you? Do you think you'll ever build here?"

Jake shrugged. "I had plans to, but things fell through."

"Why?"

"I'm not sure I want to talk about it." He lifted a corner of the quilt, twisted it between his fingers. "But I know we shouldn't keep secrets."

The words tossed Carin off kilter. How long would it be right—fair—to keep *her* secrets to herself? "You don't have to explain if you don't want to." Guilt filled her, because she said the words in part to keep herself off the hook. She wanted to know everything about Jake...yet she didn't...because that would mean sharing things about herself as well. Was she ready to open that door?

"No, it's just..." He hesitated. "I was...engaged. It didn't work out."

"Why?" One simple word—a landmine of answers.

"My schedule—and Corey—got in the way." Jake released the quilt and tugged the ball cap low over his eyes.

"The truth is it was more than tough enough being pastor of the church when I lived alone. Toss in a rambunctious kid, and you might as well ignite a case of dynamite. It has the same effect."

"Such imagery."

"Comes in handy, being a pastor—keeps the congregation listening." He ran his hands through a sea of leaves that crunched beneath his fingers. "But I'm serious. My time is never really my own. It's definitely not your typical nine-to-five job, and the money won't keep a girl in Gucci."

"Gucci?" Carin laughed at the thought. "Who cares about Gucci?"

"You?"

She shook her head. "Not in the least."

"Hmm...anyway, Corey and Rachelle were like kerosene and matches. It wasn't exactly the makings of a happily ever after."

"So you had to choose?"

Jake nodded. "But by the end it was hardly difficult."

"Maybe you should have brought Rachelle here to your wisdom tree more often, and she might have grown to know you better, and learned to love what you do, as well."

"I...never brought her here."

"No?" The admission startled Carin. "Why?"

"I'm not sure. I guess somewhere deep inside I just sensed it wasn't the right thing to do, to share this with her." Jake shook off the idea. "That sounds crazy, doesn't it?"

"Depends on your definition of crazy, I guess."

"It's a special place to me, kind of sacred, something of my own, untouched by the daily lives of others. It was selfish, wasn't it—to keep something so important from someone I was planning to share my life with?"

"There's nothing selfish about you, Jake." Carin wrapped a thread from the quilt around her finger, tugging to dispel the tension that gnawed her belly. "I'm sorry it didn't work out. I'm sorry you were hurt."

"I'm not hurt...not anymore. Dealing with the whole

situation taught me something important—to cherish what really matters."

"And what really matters is...?"

"My family...the church...my friends, and keeping Corey on the right path. He's my responsibility, and I owe it to my parents to do things right. I want to be like them and like my grandparents. I want to build a legacy of the simplest kind that will stand strong long after I'm gone."

"Hmmm..." Carin noted the determination in his gaze. It punched a hole right through the wall that eclipsed her heart. "That's very wise."

"Yeah...my wisdom tree." Jake took her hand, drew her closer. "How about you, Carin? Have you ever been serious with anyone?"

A chill washed over her. Trusting Phillip...naïvely believing he was nothing but sincere in his feelings for her, had been the worst mistake of her life. Oh, how could she have been so foolish?

"That's a story for another day. Maybe we should head back to the church. It's getting late." Carin wiggled from his touch and leaned against the tree trunk to balance as she found her footing.

"Nice move." Jake watched as she brushed grass from the seat of her jeans. "Very smooth change of subject. But I'll respect your desire not to share right now, OK?"

"Thanks. I don't want to...spoil all this." Carin swept a hand across the cloud-wisped expanse of sky.

"That bad, huh?"

"Unfortunately."

"Well, for what it's worth, I could definitely get used to sharing time with you here at the wisdom tree."

Carin's breath hitched. She swallowed hard to force back the lump that filled her throat. "That's the nicest, sweetest thing anyone's ever said to me, Jake." She hid her tears as she helped him gather the quilt. "And, for the record, I could definitely get used to it, too."

"How about we stop for some lunch on the way back?"

Jake bundled the quilt in one arm and reached for her hand. "It's way past noon, and we worked hard on the garden this morning."

"OK." Carin swiped her eyes and attempted a smile. "On one condition."

"Name it."

"I want to show you something—someone, I mean—who can use a bit of company and a nice, warm meal, too."

あぶ

"Lilly, we brought you lunch." Carin set the bucket of fried chicken on the table beside bowls of mashed potatoes smothered in gravy and buttered green beans. Warm, fluffy biscuits, and sweet tea rounded out the meal. "It's your favorite again."

"We?" Lilly gazed up from the rocking chair with crisp, gray eyes and squinted. "Who's that with you?"

"This is Jake Samuels. And he brought a friend from next door—Pastor Julian."

"Pastor Jake, from East Ridge Church?" Lilly leaned forward in the chair and set her crochet hook on her lap. "Come closer. I can't see you."

Jake removed his ball cap, took a few steps, and knelt beside the chair. The scent of spearmint gave the room a fresh feel, and he suddenly understood why Pastor Julian, whose room was just next door, often insisted his wife was close by. The spearmint scent must travel down the hall. "Here I am. Is this better?"

"Oh, much better." Lilly turned to Pastor Julian. "Now, it's your turn."

Jake eased Pastor Julian closer, and he and Lilly gaped at each other. "So, you're the lady who grows spearmint?" Pastor Julian asked.

"Sure." Lilly nodded. "You want a sprig?"

"Nothing finer. Sure, I'll have one. You got any sweet tea to go with that?"

"Right here." Carin poured a round of glasses from the jug she and Jake had brought. She handed one to Pastor Julian. "Here you go."

"What are you making?" Jake touched the tightly-stitched loops of soft pink yarn nestled on Lilly's lap and admired the handiwork. "It looks complicated."

"Nothing in life is too complicated when you take it one step at a time," Lilly assured him.

"It's a baby cap," Carin explained. "Lilly makes them for the preemies in the NICU at Children's Hospital."

"So, you're the one...I've seen the babies wearing them when I've gone to visit. I always wondered where they came from."

"Mystery solved." Lilly squinted again and placed a hand on Jake's shoulder. "Do you think you and Carin can drop them by the hospital on your way home? The lady who usually picks them up is under the weather this week, so she didn't come to get them this morning."

"Of course," Jake agreed. "We drive right by there. It's no problem at all."

"Thank you."

Carin set the dinette table with paper plates and plastic forks. "Where are your eyeglasses, Lilly? You'll need them to stitch the caps."

"I don't know. I thought I set them on the table with my Bible, but..."

"I'll mount a search," Jake offered, standing to make a round of the room. "They can't have gone too far."

"Check the trash can," Pastor Julian instructed. "I've found my fair share of lost things in the trash can."

"Come on over to the table while Jake hunts, Lilly." Carin placed the skein of yarn in the knitting bag beside the rocker and helped her from the chair. "You can drink your tea there."

Lilly tilted her head, pausing to gaze at Carin as she eased herself from the chair. "You know what I like to drink, Elise, just like your father always did. He had to go away on business again, but he'll be home Friday."

"Where did he go, Lilly?" Carin asked. Jake heard the catch in her voice and glanced over to see a shadow of sadness cross her eyes as she helped Lilly settle in at the table.

"To Nashville, of course. He always had to go to Nashville." Lilly spooned potatoes into her mouth. "We should save a piece of chicken for him, and a scoop of potatoes. He'll be home in a few days."

Carin was slow to respond. But when she did, her tone was light and even. "Of course we should. Maybe he'd like a biscuit, too?"

"Oh, yes. Biscuits are his favorite."

Jake found a trash can beside Lilly's desk. He lifted it, jostled the contents, and saw the wire-rimmed spectacles. "You were right, Pastor Julian. I found the glasses." Jake reached into the trash can. "They must have gotten mixed up with breakfast." A banana peel covered one wire arm, and Jake shook it from the metal. "I'll clean them for you, Lilly."

"See, I told you. Ava's favorite hiding place." Pastor Julian sipped his tea.

"Pastor Jake, right?" Lilly turned in her chair at the sound of his voice, and as quickly as she'd slipped away, she came back to them. But her gaze was a bit dazed, her voice hesitant. "Are you a friend of Carin's?"

"Yes," Jake said softly as he wiped the glasses with the hem of his T-shirt then handed them to Lilly. He settled in beside her near the table. "That's right. Let's eat now, OK? You don't want the food to get cold."

Lilly reached for a piece of chicken. "Did I tell you about the time Elise got into my makeup?"

"No." The worried look on Carin's face made it difficult for Jake to swallow the bite of biscuit he'd stuffed into his mouth. He chewed and washed the crumbs down with a sip of tea.

"Why don't you tell us now?" Pastor Julian urged in his gravelly voice. "Get on with it."

Lilly dug into the bowl of green beans. "She was six, I think, and school was out for the summer. Oh, I loved the summers! Elise and I had such wonderful times together playing in the sunshine. I taught her how to plant a garden and how to can squash and carrots." She slipped a forkful of green beans into her mouth. "Anyway, Elise liked to go into my room and play dress- up with my clothes and jewelry, and especially with my shoes. Those days I wore all the high heels, because they were the latest fashion and I was young and foolish." She drew a sigh. "She would put those heels on her little feet, dress herself up, and parade around the house like a movie star. I remember how the heels used to clack across the linoleum in the kitchen while I cooked dinner for Albert."

Jake could almost picture it...a little girl dreaming of the adventures to come while her mom fussed over the stove. "What happened with the makeup, Lilly?"

"Well, we were getting ready to go to the town square for the Fourth-of-July parade and fireworks show, and I thought I'd gussy myself up a little. So I had all my makeup spread out across the dresser—the lipsticks and rouges, pressed powder and eyeliner."

"Oh, no. She didn't..." Jake's words faded as he drew a breath and gathered Carin close to his side.

"Yes, she did. I was just about to paint the canvas, so to speak, when the phone rang. I went to answer it, and my Aunt Myrtle burned my ears for half an hour. By the time I got back to the bedroom—oh, boy—Elise had worn the lipsticks to tiny nubs drawing a mural of flowers across the walls. Oh, she was naughty that day! But I just couldn't be angry with her, even though I had to go to the celebration with bare lips and pale cheeks. And Albert wouldn't think of painting over the artwork. Said it added character to the room. So we slept among the flowers until Albert passed on, and I sold the house and moved away." She sighed, and her voice caught. "Oh, I miss him so."

# 11

"The sonnet is a love poem," Carin instructed her sixth-period class as she scribbled notes across the whiteboard. "It's to be filled with heartfelt emotion."

"I don't have no need for love poems," Jimmy Doyle grumbled from his seat at the back of the room. "Why do we gotta learn this stuff?"

"You *gotta*," Carin emphasized, "because, luckily, hope springs eternal for even the most undeserving of us all."

"Oh, Jimmy," Julia chimed in, "what Miss O'Malley means is you might get lucky enough to coax some girl into dating you one day, and you'll want to have a clue about how to keep her, since you probably won't be getting any second chances. Isn't that right, Miss O'Malley?"

"Thank you, Julia, for that very insightful observation." Carin switched on the overhead projector and an outline flashed across the whiteboard. "Now, as I was saying—"

"Someone's at the door, Miss O'Malley," Julia interrupted.

Carin glanced up and saw Jake through the glass. He smiled and offered a quick wave as the dismissal bell rang. The students shuffled in their seats, gathering books and backpacks, ready to bolt. Carin lifted a hand to still them. "OK, we'll discuss this further tomorrow. Remember to bring the rough draft of your sonnet to class and be prepared to share." She dropped her hand and nodded slightly. "You may go now."

Chair legs scraped against tile as students rushed for the door. Jake sidestepped and wove his way through the mass, nodding to a few of the kids he knew from church. He stopped just short of Carin's desk and grinned. "Hi. I hope I'm not interrupting."

"Not at all." Carin switched off the overhead light, leaving the fan on. "It's good to see you."

"You, too. So, you're teaching the kids how to write love poems?"

"They're going to pass love notes anyway. Might as well teach them the correct way to compose one."

"Makes sense." Jake rocked back on his heels. "I guess I'd better brush up on my technique, then."

Carin laughed. "You can always audit my class."

Jake planted a hand on her desk and leaned in. "That's nice...hearing you laugh."

"You seem to have a knack for tickling my funny bone."

"We all have our hidden talents." Jake winked. "Are you free to leave now, or do you have lessons to plan and essays to slash?"

"I have some papers to grade, but they can wait." Carin breathed in the scent of soap and aftershave, noted the pressed khakis and a navy polo that hugged his ample biceps. "I've run out of my infamous green ink, anyway."

"I came by to check on you. You were pretty upset when we left Lilly last night."

"Yeah." She followed the curve of his clean-shaven jaw, noted genuine concern in his eyes. "Sorry about that. Crying seems to be my specialty lately."

"I'd like to change that."

"Oh?" Her heart did a little two-step. "How?"

"With a dose of football, maybe some dinner afterwards."

"Football?"

"Sure. Want to head over to the ball field and catch Corey's game? They're playing the top rival this afternoon."

"Well." She remembered now that Corey had mentioned the game to her as he left class that morning. "I certainly couldn't miss that. And there *is* something I need to talk to you about."

"Such as...?"

"Not here." Carin gathered her tote and purse. "Let me put these essays in my car; then we can head to the field, if you want."

Jake nestled the stack of books she handed him in one hand and reached for her with his other. "Sounds like a plan."

❧

"What did you buy at the concession stand?" Jake asked as he spread a blanket across the concrete stadium bleacher. Carin settled in beside him, zipping her windbreaker.

"Mini peanut butter cups." The bag rustled as she opened it. "Want some?"

"They're my favorite." Jake delved into the bag and came out with a small handful. He tossed the candy into his mouth. "How did you know?"

"Corey mentioned it in his journal." Carin uncapped a bottle of water. "He wrote he has to hide them from you after you grocery shop because you'll eat the entire bag. His exact words, I believe, were, 'I didn't get any of the peanut butter cups last night because my big fat pig of a brother ate the whole bag before I had a chance to hide them.'"

Jake paused mid-bite. "He wrote that?"

Carin handed him the bag. "Uh-huh. Direct quote."

"Hmm...the little rat." Jake settled into the bleacher beside her and scanned the field below. Corey was passing a football to a teammate during a pre-game drill. "I think maybe it's time to keep a journal of my own."

"I encourage the writing process in just about any capacity." Carin sipped water. "The pen is mightier than the sword, and all that."

"Yeah, well my pen is an entire army, and I'll slay anyone who tries to get his grubby hands on my peanut butter cups."

"I won't touch them." Carin laughed. "I promise. I'll stick to my popcorn."

"You're exempted from the rule." Jake offered her the bag. "I'll share with you."

"That's nice, because I like them, too." She took a cup. "May I ask you a question, Jake?"

"Ask away."

"Hailey wants me to help her teach the middle-grades Sunday school class, and we thought we'd encourage the kids to help with the memory garden, too…like I mentioned to you."

"That's not a question."

"I know. But what do you think…about me?"

"I think you're lovely." He grazed her chin with his knuckle.

"No. I mean, what do you think about me *here*." She pressed her palm to her chest. "In my heart?"

"I'm not sure I understand what you're asking."

"Let me rephrase." She wiggled closer to him and reached into the candy bag for another piece of chocolate. "Were you nervous the first time you got up in front of a church to speak?"

"Oh, I was scared to death." Jake remembered the Sunday clearly. As he'd approached the pulpit, he felt as if a million pairs of eyes swept over him. His heart took off at sprint-speed, and he thought, for a fleeting moment, that he might fall flat on his face. "East Ridge Church presented a tough crowd. Some of the older parishioners felt I was too young to lead a church, and they didn't hesitate to make their views known. I felt like I was under a microscope for a while, and it was so hard. Mr. Staley and his wife took me under their wing and made me feel welcome. Mrs. Staley was still alive then and very active in the church."

"What was she like?"

"She had a beautiful spirit. She didn't let everyday frustrations get her down. She had a stronger faith than anyone I've ever known."

"That's what everyone says."

"The cancer claimed her so fast we barely had time to fathom it. Mr. Staley took her passing pretty hard. We thought we'd lose him, too, but God has a way of providing the strength and desire for a person to take one more step even when he's convinced he can't."

"I believe that."

"After my parents died, most of the older folks began to accept me. It was a rite of passage, I suppose, to lose my mom and dad. It presented a measure of maturity I couldn't turn my back on."

"You hardly had a choice."

"You should help Hailey teach the class, Carin." Jake nodded. "You have a lot to offer our kids."

"But I'm not sure...I don't know." She shook her head. "My faith isn't very strong, to say the least."

"That's even more reason, then. I'm sure you understand that sometimes teaching others teaches us as well."

"That's true. You're right, Jake."

"Now, I have something to ask you—a favor."

"If you want me to mow the church lawn for you, you can forget it."

"No." Jake laughed. "The mower's retired for another season."

"Then what kind of favor do you need?"

"A chaperone."

"What kind of chaperone?"

"For the amusement park. Patrick and Julie and I are taking the youth group next Saturday, and we can use another set of eyes. It would give you a chance to get to know the kids, too, before you start to help Hailey with the class."

"You mean you want me to spend the day riding roller coasters and the Ferris wheel with a bunch of screaming teenagers?"

"Well, I was hoping I might talk you into riding the Ferris wheel with *me*, but you have the general idea."

"OK, I'll go if you promise not to rock the wheel's seat while we're stopped at the top."

"If you ride with me, I promise to be a complete gentleman." His tone teased.

"Are you crossing your fingers behind your back?"

"No. I wouldn't do that…at least as far as you know."

"OK, I'll go. But you'd better not scream like a girl flying down those humongous hills on the coasters."

"Like a girl? Oh, you wound me." Jake splayed a palm across his chest.

"Corey told me you don't much like heights…or roller coasters."

"The little rat. What else has he told you about me?"

"Oh, he's just a fount of information."

"I'll bet. You shouldn't believe half of what he writes."

"Even so, that still leaves plenty."

"That does it. Tonight he's getting a plate of lima beans for dinner and absolutely no dessert—no dessert at all."

# 12

"Let's hit Thunder River first." Corey wove his way through the crowd toward the hulking steel coaster. "There's not much of a line."

"I don't know…" Jake gazed up at the massive and unforgiving twists and turns of the track. Shrieks drifted on the breeze like confetti, and the wheels roared against winding metal. "It's the biggest ride in the park. Maybe we should work our way up to it, warm up a little first."

"What, and give you a chance to chicken out? Forget that idea." Corey clutched Jake's arm. "It's more fun this way. You gotta plunge right in—enjoy the full effect."

"It's that effect I'm worried about." Jake cringed. "I'm just being…cautious."

"Well, you can be cautious from thirty stories up. Just close your eyes and remember to breathe so you don't hyperventilate."

"Great. Thanks for the visualization. I feel so much better now."

"Come on." Carin grinned at Jake. "I'll ride with you and hold your hand."

"Well, I can't pass up an offer like that."

"Oh, look." Corey pointed toward the tracks. "The bottom of the coaster drops out when you get to the top of the first massive hill, just before you fall, so your legs dangle free. All that's keeping you from hurtling into space is the shoulder harness. That's so cool!"

Jake blanched. "If this ride breaks down while we're on it and we get stuck upside down in one of those inverted loops, none of you is ever going to hear the end of it."

"Get real, Jake." Corey rolled his eyes. "It's not going to break down. They do safety checks, you know. You're gonna love it."

"Like a root canal."

∂∞∾

"Let's take a break." Jake said much later, as they wound their way through a dwindling crowd. "How about some ice cream?" He turned to Carin, grinning wearily. "What do you like, Miss Mario...as in Andretti?"

She loved speed—he'd learned that pretty quickly. First seat, last seat, or somewhere in the middle—it didn't matter as long as the coaster flew over the tracks at death-defying speeds. And the array of loops and swirls made the ride even better. Even so, she'd taken pity on Jake and called for the bumper cars when it was her turn to choose a ride.

"Hmm..." Carin peered through the glass display case at the colorful tubs of ice cream. "All those dips and turns *did* make me awfully hungry." She tapped the glass. "A double-scoop strawberry cheesecake swirl ought to put a dent in things."

"Strawberry cheesecake swirl, coming up." Jake ordered two, and then left the kids to place their orders while he and Carin settled at a table out on the veranda.

"I'm surprised you can eat that." Carin watched Jake bite into his cone. "You look like you're just beginning to recover from the most horrendous case of the flu."

Jake paused mid-bite and grimaced. "That bad, huh?"

"Yeah. White as a sheet doesn't begin to cover it." She nibbled a bite of strawberry. "Why did you come here today if you don't like the rides so much? There had to be someone else from the church that would have chaperoned in your place."

"I came because Corey loves the rides, and he loves coming to places like this. I figure, he puts up with a lot of pretty boring stuff because of me, so the least I can do is suffer through a few rides…toss my lunch a few times…lose my voice hollering like a girl—"

"You haven't hollered even once."

"I know." He tugged the collar of his T-shirt. "And the restraint is killing me."

Carin laughed. "You're an amazing brother, Jake."

"I just take one small step at a time, count to ten a lot."

"Yeah, those teenage years can really do a person in."

"No kidding. I'm developing the gray hair to prove it."

"I don't see any gray hair."

"Look closer." He pulled her toward him, fought the urge to kiss her. The pastor in him said it was wrong…in front of so many kids. But the man in him searched for an excuse to devour her.

"What are you doing?" Corey fell into a chair at their table, breaking the mood. "You have something in your hair, Jake?"

*So much for snatching a kiss.* Jake sighed. "Yeah, a whole lot of gray." He finished the last bite of his cone and stood. "I can see our little siesta has come to an abrupt end. It's getting dark. Why don't we head over to the Ferris wheel?"

"Sounds great." Carin gathered her fanny pack. "Something a bit slower paced is just what the doctor ordered after that ice cream."

"Yeah, if you're middle-aged." Corey groaned.

"Who are you calling middle-aged?" Jake thumped Corey on the back. "Nobody here is even close to middle-aged—not yet, anyway. It's my turn to choose a ride, and I choose the wheel."

"OK. I don't need a lecture." Corey wiggled from his touch.

"Then get walking—double-time."

The group rounded a corner to see the Ferris wheel soar. Lights illuminated each spoke of the wheel, outlining it against a star-studded, velvet sky. The seats were open, and feet dangled from above as the wheel spun.

"It doesn't look so wimpy at night," Corey commented.

"OK, I guess it'll be fun to ride."

"Glad I have your stamp of approval." Jake took Carin's hand. "Pair up."

The line was short, so they chose partners and piled into seats.

"Look." Jake nudged Carin's shoulder and pointed to the seat below. "Corey and Amy are riding together. And Dillon and Carla. We'll have to keep our eyes on them."

"It doesn't mean anything, really." Carin slipped into a seat and scooted over to make room for Jake. "It's just very uncool for two guys to ride the Ferris wheel together, so they're riding with the girls. That's all."

"Is that your excuse for riding with me?"

"Would you rather have Patrick ride shotgun?"

"I don't think Julie would like that."

Carin grinned as they went into motion. "Remember your promise not to rock the seat."

"What promise?" Jake winked and gave the seat a gentle nudge. "I don't remember any promise."

"Jake!"

"Just kidding. You're safe with me."

The wheel paused with their seat at the top, affording an amazing view of the park below. Illuminated rides glimmered in the darkness like a sea of colorful stars.

"Did we really ride that coaster?" Jake watched the cars speed through an inverted loop, glittering in the blanket of darkness. Faint squeals and laughter whispered across the breeze.

"Yes, we did." Carin massaged her knuckles. "And I have the bruised hand to prove it."

"I'm sorry." Jake twined his fingers with hers to stroke bruises away with the pad of his thumb. "I didn't mean to squeeze so tight."

"It's OK. We shouldn't have made you ride so many coasters. I guess that wasn't a very nice thing to do."

"If I had a journal, I'd document my angst." He lifted his free hand, as if scrawling across the darkness. "But now that it's over, I'm glad I rode them all. It's a better fate than spending the next month taking jabs from the kids."

"They can be brutal, can't they? Some days I feel like pulling my hair out and trading teaching for a greeter job at the local home improvement store." Carin tugged a curl, grimacing. "But I sure missed teaching while I was away from it."

"While you helped your dad?"

"Yes. I really missed teaching."

"Yeah, the cafeteria food...spit balls flying across the classroom...parents complaining...kids passing notes—um, I mean sonnets."

"I could say the same about you, Preacher Man. Mowing the lawn in the scalding heat of summer...emergency phone calls in the middle of the night...sermons, sermons, and more sermons...kids hiding the sanctuary flowers so the altar is bare when the service begins...need I say more?"

"I guess we both have our moments."

"Yes, we do. But I wouldn't trade it, and I gather you wouldn't, either." The breeze tangled Carin's hair, and she brushed a curl from her face and leaned against Jake, pressing her cheek to his arm. "Thank you, Jake."

"For what?"

"For asking me to come today."

"You've had fun?"

"Yes. Definitely. I don't want the day to end."

"I don't, either." Jake shifted in the seat, drawing her close. "Would you mind...if I stole a kiss?"

She tilted her head, offering her lips. "I thought you'd never ask."

⮞⮜

"Thanks for driving me home," Carin said as Jake pulled up to the house. "But you should just let me out here at the road. It's late, and you'll be tired for church in the morning."

"Never too late to walk you to the door." He turned into

the drive and switched off the ignition. The driver's door popped as he pulled the latch. "Wait there. I'll come around."

"It was nice of Patrick and Julie to take Corey home with them again." Carin slipped from the seat as he opened the passenger door. The night air made her shiver, and Jake eased an arm around her shoulders as they made their way up the walk.

"Yeah. It was the perfect ending to a great day for the boys—getting to hang out together tonight, too."

"I'll bet they won't sleep a wink."

"Probably not."

She gathered the seam of her windbreaker and glanced toward the house. She gasped when she saw a light in the living room window. "Jake, wait." She pointed. "Look."

"What?" He turned in the direction she motioned. "You mean the light? Didn't you leave it on?"

"No." Carin shook her head. Her bones turned to ice. "I didn't."

"Are you sure?"

"Yes, Jake. Look by the door." The planter beside the door was toppled, and potting soil covered the welcome mat. She remembered the key she'd hidden beneath the ceramic pot— the same hiding place she'd used at her apartment in Nashville. Only two people knew that hiding place—and she'd spoken to her dad just that morning.

"Maybe Scooter got loose and he bumped into it?"

"He was eating when we left, remember?"

"Were you expecting company?"

Unable to speak, Carin shook her head slowly.

"OK. Stay here." Jake's tone left no room for discussion. "Get back in the Jeep and wait."

Terror coursed through Carin as Jake stepped in front of her, shielding her from the house.

She placed a hand on his back. "Jake, don't go—"

"It's OK." He gave her a nudge toward the driveway. "Just get back in the Jeep."

"I can't." Her breath caught as a shadow crossed the

living room window. "I won't let you go in there alone."

"What are you doing?" Jake spun to face her as she slipped around him. "This is no time to be stubborn."

"I think…" The shadow crossed the window once more, and she was certain. "I mean I know who it is."

"Who?"

The front door flew open, startling her, and Phillip stepped onto the porch. His hands clenched into fists as the light of a full moon washed over him.

"Hello, Carin." His shoulders tensed to match the menacing tone of his voice. "It's been too long, hasn't it?"

A scream died in Carin's throat as Jake stepped in front of her, shielding her from Phillip like a towering concrete wall.

"Who are you?" Jake's voice rang low, the tone calm, but Carin heard the edge to it and knew instinctively that he'd protect her at all cost.

Phillip took a step forward so the security light over the front door illuminated his face. "I should ask you the same." Onyx eyes glittered like a tiger's, and his features were sharp and menacing as they zeroed in on Carin. "Care to explain what this other guy's doing here—with you—after midnight and heading into your house?"

She smelled the alcohol on his breath. "I don't owe you an explanation of any kind." Her voice trembled over each word.

"I disagree." Phillip took a step toward her, his hands coming up, and Carin nestled closer to Jake. "It's been too long. We need to talk."

"Don't come any closer." Carin shook her head. "You need to leave."

"Go, Carin." Jake handed her his cell phone and then pushed her back—away from the light, away from Phillip—so she stumbled into the grass. "Go next door. Call the police."

"Please, Phillip, just leave," Carin pleaded. "Haven't you done enough, caused enough trouble?"

Jake took a step forward, approaching Phillip. "You heard her. She wants you to leave."

"I'm not going anywhere." Phillip slouched against the

porch rail and lifted a cigarette to his lips, then reached into the pocket of his slacks and pulled out a lighter.

Soon the tip of the cigarette glowed orange-red and smoke billowed around his head. His gaze locked on Carin. "I want to talk to you, Carin." The tone of his voice escalated a notch, and Carin knew he was agitated. If this continued, he'd soon lose control.

Carin shook her head. "Just go find a place to sleep it off and—and maybe—"

"I'd like to sleep it off here." His grin was menacing. "With you. Now that I've had a little taste—"

"No!" Chills coursed through Carin, and her teeth began to chatter. She rubbed her arms as a sob escaped her lips. "Never."

"Do you want him to leave, Carin?" Jake asked without turning to face her.

"Yes."

"Then go next door and let me handle this."

She pressed a fist to her lips and backpedaled, nodding as the tears came. Would this nightmare ever end?

Her fingers trembled on Jake's cell phone as she ran toward the neighbor's house. A quick rap on the front door, and she was ushered inside by Mrs. Malloy. Carin handed her the cell phone.

"Please, call the police." She doubled over, struggling to breathe. Afraid for Jake's safety, she began to pray.

Suddenly sirens wailed down the street, and Carin rushed to the front window. Phillip ran toward the corner, leaping a hedgerow. Voices shouted. Feet pounded the pavement, and two police officers tackled Phillip to the ground as he crossed beneath a streetlight.

Phillip bellowed as an officer cuffed him and began to recite his Miranda rights.

Jake took one look at Carin, drew her close, and held her. "It's OK now."

She collapsed into his arms, sobbing as pent up fear finally found its way to the surface. "I'm sorry, Jake."

*"You're* sorry." He rubbed her back gently as he pressed his lips to her ear. "What did he do to you, Carin?"

# 13

"Do you want some coffee?" Carin came to her doorway and surveyed the array of tools and hardware Jake had spread across the porch. She'd changed out of her church clothes and into jeans and a white cotton blouse, and her curls were brushed back into a ponytail.

Jake knew she hadn't slept at all after the police hauled the thug named Phillip off in a cruiser. She'd sat stoically through church, her fingers clasped tightly in her lap. His gut clenched every time he looked at her, each time he saw the dark shadows of hurt that marred her pretty green eyes.

He wanted to take that guy's—Phillip's—head right off his shoulders. He'd hurt Carin bad, Jake was sure of it. She didn't need to tell him. He already knew. And the fact that he felt such a twist in his belly every time he thought of the fear in Carin's eyes and the way she'd cowered the moment she saw Phillip through her living room window made Jake realize just how human he was.

"Jake?" Carin waved a hand in front of his eyes. "Are you OK?"

"Sorry." He lifted his head to meet her gaze. "No, thanks on the coffee. I want to get this finished."

She stepped onto the porch and leaned against the rail. "I appreciate you doing this...changing the locks for me. Maybe Phillip didn't take the key with him, but the planter where I hid it is cracked and the key's missing, so he probably did." She shook her head, her cheeks turning a shade or two pastier. "I should have chosen a different hiding place. That's the same one I used in Nashville, so he knew..."

"It's OK. It can't be undone now, and I don't mind putting

in the new locks. It's not hard." Jake reached for a screwdriver. "But I'm worried about you. How are you holding up?"

"I'm OK." She pulled the collar of her blouse tight as the breeze kicked up. Colorful leaves tumbled along the grass in the front yard, spreading their musky scent. "How about you? You didn't sleep much last night."

"I'm holding up all right. I'll feel better when this lock and the one on the back door are changed. Patrick's working on that one right now."

"I know. And Julie's inside fussing over dinner while the boys are out back, searching for Scooter."

"Any luck?"

"No." Carin caught her lower lip between her teeth and shook her head. "Not yet."

"They'll find him." Jake took the pieces of the new door handle from its wrapping and began to mount the guts of it to the solid-oak front door. "But I wish this door was metal. I don't like the idea of that creep getting into your house again."

"He won't...not after you finish replacing those locks. And I imagine the police had a pretty good talk with him, after you came back here last night."

"I imagine they did." Jake's gut burned. An officer had shared some basic details, but from the sound of things, Jake was pretty sure Phillip wouldn't try to come around again. "No more hiding an extra key. I can hold one for you...or Hailey or Julie, if you'd rather."

"I can't believe Julie and Patrick showed up here today after church with a roast and all the trimmings."

"They're worried about you. They don't like this any more than I do."

"I'm not used to people fussing over me."

"It's what we do when we care about someone. And you're one of us now, like it or not."

"But they shouldn't...care about me, I mean. I'm bad publicity for your church—and for you, Jake."

"You're no such thing." Jake reached for a screw, examined it before slipping it into a metal plate along the doorframe. "That's nonsense."

"It's the truth."

"OK." He spoke without looking at her, trying hard to keep his temper in check. One glance at the sleep-shadowed eyes, the pale skin, and he'd be in his Jeep, on his way to Nashville, to hunt the bully named Phillip. And where would that get any of them? "So what you're saying is, you don't deserve to be cared for by people who are beginning to love you, but you *do* deserve to be pushed around, made to endure threats, and God only knows what else, by someone who doesn't?"

Carin shoved away from the rail and began to pace the length of the porch. "No. Of course not. It's just…"

"Let Julie fuss. Her roast will melt in your mouth."

"Do you think Phillip will come back, Jake?"

"He'd better not." Jake tossed the screwdriver down, reached for needle-nose pliers. "But it would certainly help if you'd agree to file a restraining order."

"I know. But it's sure to get back to my dad, since he and Phillip still work together. And I don't want to upset him…or worry him." She fidgeted, her lower lip trembling.

"Don't you think your father should know what kind of creep he has working for him? I don't have to tell you, the guy's dangerous, Carin. He could have hurt you last night. What if I hadn't been here? What if you'd come home alone?"

"I don't want to think…" Her voice cracked, and Jake turned to see her press a hand to her mouth, her fingers trembling. "I'm scared, but I can't let it paralyze me." Tears magnified her eyes, spilling down her cheeks.

Jake stood to gather her into his arms. "You don't have to do this alone. I'm here now. Let me help you."

Carin pressed her face to his T-shirt, and he stroked her hair. She trembled against him, and he knew she was fighting to keep the tears in check. "It's too complicated."

"Nothing's too complicated. We just need to talk it out. I'm starting to care for you, Carin, and it's killing me to see you hurting. And I don't even know *why* you're hurting. What happened?" Jake murmured into her hair. "Last night...well, you were upset and I understand why you didn't want to discuss it. But now..."

"I'm...sorry, Jake." Carin disengaged herself from his embrace and stepped back, crossing her arms. "I shouldn't have dragged you into this."

"Stop, please. You didn't drag me into anything." He placed his hands on her shoulders and held her gaze. "I want this—want you—of my own free will."

"But—"

"I'd like to know what happened—what Phillip did to you so I know what I'm up against." Jake nodded sharply. "If you won't protect yourself, then I'll do it for you."

"I don't want you to have to protect me. It's not your job."

"Too late."

"I'll file a restraining order, Jake, and I'm going to tell my dad about this...along with a few other things. I promise— soon."

"Hey, you two." Julie came to the doorway, an apron tied around her waist to protect her pretty linen dress. "Dinner's ready. Come in and wash up."

Carin loosened her crossed arms and reached for Jake's hand. "We can discuss this more later, if you'd like."

He nodded. "Oh, I'd like."

She swiped tears from her eyes and turned toward Julie. "I'll come help you," she offered. "I'll set the table."

"It's already done. The boys just took care of it. I think they have an internal food radar. As soon as they smelled the gravy, they came running. They're already at the table, washed and chomping at the bit. Patrick, too. He's finished replacing the lock on the back door."

"Good, so they're both done, now." Jake breathed a sigh of relief. "I'll rest better tonight knowing that."

"Now, if we could just find Scooter. He must have run away when Phillip opened the front door. He's not used to being outside. What if he gets lost...or scared?" Carin said as she shivered, and Jake wondered what made her feel so cold—

the breeze or worry over the cat she'd grown to love.

"We'll find him." Jake pulled her in and held her tucked up against his chest. He pressed his lips to the crown of her head, inhaling the sweet berry scent of her shampoo. The tension in his belly kicked up a notch as he felt her tremble. He had to trust she had her reasons for being a bit evasive. Lord knows he'd grown weary of repeating the details of his parents' death over the months that followed. Each retelling opened the wound, made it that much harder to heal.

"It's going to be OK."

"You don't know that…not for sure."

"I know it the best I can. We've got God on our side, Carin. There's no stronger or more faithful warrior."

"But what about Scooter?" She sniffled.

"We'll continue the search as soon as we're done with dinner."

"OK."

Jake released her and took her by the hand. He skimmed a hand across her cheek and then bowed to kiss her before they went into the house.

Corey glanced up from the kitchen table when they strode through the doorway. "We're going to look more for Scooter," he shared as he filled glasses with sweet tea. "Dillon thinks he might be hiding in a tree in the woods.

"Yeah," Dillon chimed in from beside Corey at the table. "I have a friend whose cat got stuck in a tree, and he stayed there almost a week before they found him."

"Oh, no." Carin's voice cracked. "Was he OK?"

"After eating a mountain of tuna, yeah," Corey said.

Jake turned from the table as the patter of tiny feet scurried behind him.

"Hi, Uncle Jake." Patrick and Julie's youngest, Gracie, raced over to hug Jake's legs. Even though Jake wasn't really her uncle, she'd called him that the first time he had dinner at their house, more than two years ago, and the name stuck.

"Hi, princess. I heard you have a birthday coming up."

"Uh-huh." She stepped back to hold up a hand with all

five fingers splayed. "I'm gonna be this many."

"Twenty-seven?"

"No, silly." Her copper-colored hair, the same shade as Julie's, danced in baby-fine curls around her freckled face. "Five."

"Oh, right." Jake tickled her belly, eliciting a round of giggles. "And what do you want for your birthday?"

"A puppy."

"Oh, my." Jake glanced up at Patrick, who shook his head as if to say, "Don't egg her on."

"What else?"

"Nothing. Just a puppy with lots of whiskers and big, floppy ears."

"Well...your dad will have to get working on that."

"Miss Carin?" She glanced up at Carin with round, dark eyes. "Do you have a puppy?"

"No. Just Scooter, my cat."

"Oh, yeah. But he ran away. I heard Corey and Dillon calling for him. I wanted to look for him, too, but Mama needed me to help her in the kitchen instead."

"I'll bet you're a good helper." Carin tapped Gracie's nose. "Did you stir the potatoes?"

"Uh-huh, and I got to sprinkle pepper on the green beans, too." Gracie puffed out her chest. "Mama and Daddy say I'm a real good helper, and sometimes even Dillon. But mostly he just yells at me when I try to go in his room."

"Gracie, do you want milk or juice?" Julie chimed in.

"Milk, Mama." Gracie eased onto her tiptoes and tugged the hem of Carin's blouse. "Does Scooter run away a lot?"

"No." Carin shook her head. "Never."

An alarm sounded in Jake's head. He feared the cat hadn't run away, but that something else—much worse—might have happened. Carin told him how much Scooter disliked Phillip.

"Well, when Scooter comes home, can I play with him?" Gracie's voice broke into Jake's thoughts.

"He'd like that."

"Hey, Mama, did you hear that? Miss Carin said I can

play with Scooter." Gracie clapped her hands. "I wonder if Scooter will be friends with my puppy, too."

"I heard." Julie wiped her hands on her apron then handed Carin a bowl of potatoes to set on the table while Patrick finished carving the roast. "Now, find a place at the table. Dinner's ready."

"OK, Mama." Gracie scrambled into a chair. "Sit next to me, Miss Carin. I want you to help me pick a name for my puppy."

∂∽⌒

Gracie's precious chatter was just the medicine Carin needed to take her mind off all the bad things—even if just for a while.

"Does Scooter like mice?" Gracie twirled her napkin around one finger.

"I suppose so." Carin shrugged. "I haven't seen any around the house."

"What does he eat?" She propped her chin on an upturned palm and leaned closer, chewing a mouthful of potatoes.

"Food from a little can—turkey and chicken livers and things like that."

"Chicken livers." The tiny mouth drew into a pucker. "Yuck."

"To Scooter they're like candy," Jake informed the child.

"But not to me. No, sir." Gracie shook her head vigorously and turned back to Carin. "Do you play with Scooter lots?"

"Sure. He has a little ball with bells inside that he likes to chase. And he likes yarn, too."

"Just like in the books Mama reads to me." Gracie scooped another spoonful of mashed potatoes into her mouth while avoiding the small pile of green beans on her plate. "The cats always like balls of yarn."

Carin pushed the food around her plate then forced down a small bite of baby carrots. She didn't want to seem unappreciative of the time Julie took to cook, yet her stomach was so tied in knots it had little room for anything else.

"You don't have to eat, Carin." Julie seemed to sense her dilemma. "It's no problem to wrap up your plate and save it for later. Maybe then you'll feel a little better."

"What's wrong, Miss Carin?" Gracie's maple-syrup eyes radiated innocence. "You don't feel good? Or maybe you miss Scooter?"

"I do miss him."

Grace sighed.

"He's been gone the whole night and all day, too." Carin dabbed at her eyes.

"We'll keep looking, Miss O'Malley." Corey dropped his napkin onto his plate. "We're done eating."

"What about the apple pie?" Julie asked, pointing toward the oven where it was warming. "Don't you want a slice?"

"I'll take a slice," Patrick chimed in. "I know better than to pass up your apple pie, honey."

"We'll get ours later." Corey pushed his chair away from the table, joined by Dillon. "After we look some more."

"I'll come, too." Jake wiped his mouth with his napkin and drained his glass of iced tea. He took the ball cap from the floor beneath his chair and tugged it down tight over the crown of his head. "Come on, boys."

"I should stay behind and help Julie clean up." Carin surveyed the mess of dishes across the table. "It looks like a war zone in here."

"I'll help," Patrick offered. "Nothing I like better than washing dishes with my beautiful wife."

Julie leaned in to kiss him. "That's what I like to hear, but why don't you help Jake and the boys, instead?"

"If you insist." Patrick kissed his wife back—square on the mouth—before she turned to run water in the sink.

"Ugh...totally disgusting." Dillon's chair legs scraped the tile. "I'm outta here. C'mon, Corey."

Patrick's laughter followed the boys out the door. "Wait for me."

# 14

Moonlight filtered through the bedroom window as Jake rested in a chair, watching the gentle rise and fall of Corey's chest beneath a comforter. The kid finally slept, the worst of the nightmares passed. They'd returned this night with a vengeance, and Jake was glad the bout was over.

Now that he had time to think about it, Jake wasn't sure how they'd overlooked Scooter. The cat wasn't found until that evening, after he and Carin, along with Corey, returned to Carin's house after church.

But Jake would always remember the sound Carin made when she first saw the poor cat lying there in the front flower bed, just to the right of the steps, partially covered with wind-blown leaves.

"Jake, oh, no." Her voice caught on a sob, and he rushed to her side. One glance told him Scooter was in dire straits. The cat's rear leg was twisted at an odd angle, the once-sleek gray fur stiff and matted with mulch.

"Don't look, Carin." Jake stepped in front of her to shield her as he knelt among the mums for a closer look. Scooter's body felt cold, and Jake was surprised to hear a faint yelp when he touched the injured leg. He slipped from his jacket and spread it over the ground, lifting Scooter and bundling him in the fabric. "He's freezing, and he needs a vet, quick. Even with that, I'm not sure…"

"Let me hold him" Carin fell to the ground beside Jake, a fist pressed to her lips. "He must have been here for hours. How did we miss him?"

"I don't know." Jake drew his car keys from his pocket. "I'll grab Corey, and we'll head to the vet. Take Scooter,

Carin."

"Phillip did this…" Carin let out a sob as she carefully nestled Scooter in her arms. "He knew it would hurt me. Oh, Jake…"

Jake's gut twisted and his shoulders tensed at the sound of Phillip's name. His need to protect Carin kicked in, and he took her hand and led her toward the Jeep, calling for Corey as they stumbled along.

Once she'd buckled in, Scooter bundled on her lap, Jake raced toward the house and up the stairs. A fine drizzle of rain began to fall, dampening the ground and chilling him through the thin fabric of his cotton T-shirt.

"Corey!" Jake hollered, gathering Carin's purse from the coffee table. "Come quick."

Corey rushed into the living room, carrying his journal. "What's the matter?"

"We found Scooter." Jake swiped damp hair from his eyes and brushed drops of rain from his arms.

"Is he OK?"

"He's…hurt pretty bad."

Corey tossed the journal onto the coffee table and strode toward the front door. "Where is he?"

"In the Jeep with Carin. We have to get him to the vet hospital *now*."

"Let's go." Corey's shoes slapped concrete as he slammed the front door and raced Jake down the stairs. "Did that guy do it—the mean dude who broke in last night?"

"We don't have proof, but Carin thinks so…and I do, too."

"What are you gonna do, Jake?"

Jake rounded the car and slipped into the driver's seat as Corey scrambled into the back. "I don't know, but I'll figure it out."

"Why would anyone want to hurt him?" In the rearview mirror, Jake saw Corey's lip tremble, and tears flooded his eyes. "He's just a cat…he didn't bother anyone."

"I don't know." Jake slipped a key into the ignition and

cranked the engine.

"Scooter's not whimpering anymore, Jake." Carin gathered the mass of fur to her chest. "I think he stopped breathing."

"No!" Corey sniffled, and his tears splashed the leather upholstery. "Hurry, Jake."

In the distance, thunder rumbled. Rain splattered the Jeep, making it hard to see the road as Jake backed from the drive. A stiff wind tossed leaves along the grass.

Jake floored the gas and headed north toward the vet hospital while Carin's sobs tore his heart to shreds.

"He's not going to make it, Jake." Tears slipped down her cheeks.

"We're almost there. It's just around the corner." Jake placed a hand on her shoulder. "Pray, OK...just pray."

A flash of lightning drew Jake back to Corey's bedroom. He sipped from a cup of coffee and read his Bible by the glow of a nightlight, much as he'd done in the first days and weeks after Corey came to live with him.

The chair belonged to his mom—she used to rock him in it, and then Corey, when they were babies. Dad had bought it when they found out she was pregnant...his first gift to her for their baby. Now Jake found a bit of comfort in the cadence, a connection to the past that offered a bit of strength.

Nausea filled him as he thought of how Carin's sobs battled the rain as they waited for word on Scooter. The veterinarian had whisked the poor cat straight to surgery that seemed to go on for hours.

When he'd finally emerged from the surgery suite, Carin stood, her shoulders heaving. "Is Scooter...is he...?"

"It will be touch and go for the next twelve hours or so"—the vet nodded—"but he came through the surgery just fine. I have high hopes."

"Thank you." She could barely speak as she slipped an index finger into her mouth and gnawed her nail.

Corey stepped forward, his T-shirt still damp from the rain. "Can we see him?"

"Not tonight." The vet glanced away long enough to jot a note on the file attached to a clipboard. "He needs to rest. But you can come back in the morning. By then, the anesthesia should be out of his system and he'll be on the mend."

"I'm not leaving." Corey crossed his arms. "I'm going to wait right here."

"Corey, you need to rest, too." Carin turned to him and brushed his hair back. She cupped his cheek with her palm, much the way their mom had. The gesture was so maternal it stole Jake's breath. Corey's eyes flashed, and Jake knew then just how much he missed their mother's gentle touch. Carin swiped tears from her face as strands of hair clung to her cheeks and curled over her shoulders. "We'll all go home and come back in the morning, OK?"

"Well…if you think that's best." Corey nodded. "I guess it's OK."

Thunder rumbled and shook the house, drawing Jake back once more. Corey rolled over in the bed, groaning, as Jake nudged the rocker harder. He wondered if Carin was faring any better in the sleep department. Jake was loath to leave her after they'd left the veterinary hospital, but she had insisted. What would people say if he spent the night—even if all he did was sleep on the living room couch?

He didn't really care what anyone thought, but he *did* care about Carin…very much. Now, all he had to do was figure out what came next.

æ

Carin sat at the kitchen table beneath a soft glow of light, sipping coffee and flipping through the Bible Jake had given her. Every creak of the floorboards or brush of a tree branch against the house jolted her senses to full alert. What if Phillip decided to return?

Scooter's dish sat empty by the French doors, eliciting a sob as her gaze was drawn to it. He might never come home again—ever.

*Just like Cameron and Mom.*

The thought brought a lump to her throat, and she forced down a sip of lukewarm coffee, wishing she'd let Jake sleep on the couch after all. They'd probably all be better off rest-wise, since she guessed he wasn't getting so much as a nap at his own house, either.

What was she doing here—in the middle of this mess? How had it happened? She didn't have an answer, but one thing she did know for sure was that it wasn't fair to Jake—or Corey, for that matter. Corey was torn up, sobbing like a baby while he watched Jake hand Scooter to the vet. The tears in his eyes made Carin want to wrap her arms around him and hug him tight, just like her own mom used to hold her.

She cared for Corey, felt a need to protect him much as she had Cameron. But even more than that, she was falling in love with Jake. She knew it as sure as she knew who'd injured Scooter.

Something inside her snapped, and she knew what she had to do. Things had gone far enough, and people were hurt. She couldn't do anything about that now, but she *could* do something about the future...*her* future...before she lost everything—everyone—she loved, again.

# 15

"Here's your journal." Carin leaned back in her desk chair and handed Corey the notebook he'd left on her living room couch yesterday. The school was quiet, except for the hum of the floor-polisher down the hall. "I…didn't read it, and you can wait until tomorrow to turn it in."

"Thanks." They had an agreement. He'd hand in the journal at the end of class each Monday, and only then would Carin read what he wrote. That way, if he jotted something in anger or frustration and then wanted to delete it by tearing out the page and writing something else instead, he'd have the weekend to mull it over. "I appreciate it."

"Where's Amy today?" Carin glanced at the clock above the classroom door. The school day had ended nearly two hours ago, and she assumed Corey had doubled back to the classroom following football practice. His hair was damp, and he'd slung his equipment bag over one shoulder. "I missed seeing her second period."

"She has a cold, so her mom kept her home. She'll probably be back tomorrow, but I can drop by her house and take her homework if you want."

"That would be nice." Carin jotted a quick note on a memo pad, then tore off the sheet and handed it to Corey. "Here you go. She'll need her grammar workbook, so if you know her lock combination you might want to stop by her locker on your way out and get it. And please tell her I hope she feels better."

"I will." He juggled his loaded backpack with the equipment bag. "Jake should be here soon, but I wanted a minute to talk to you if you…have the time."

"Of course I have the time." Carin dropped her pen and motioned to him to have a seat at the desk nearest hers. "What's on your mind?"

"Lots of things." He unloaded his equipment bag and then his backpack onto the floor beside the desk. "I'm really sorry about Scooter, but I'm glad he's going to be OK."

"Thanks. It's been nice of Jake to check on him during the day while we're at school. The doctor said he'll heal fine, but it's going to take a while." Carin set aside a handful of essays, forcing away the sadness that swept through. She fought to keep a tremor from her voice. "I'm so thankful you were there to help Jake. I don't think I could have...I know I couldn't have—it was awful to see Scooter hurting so."

"No problem. I understand. I wanted to help." Corey swiped shaggy hair from his eyes to look at her. "Jake said the guy who broke into your house probably hurt Scooter. Why would anyone want to do *that*?"

"He's not...a very nice person."

"I figured as much." Corey leaned back in the seat and stretched his legs. "But why would he want to hurt you?"

"Because I wouldn't give him what he wanted."

"What did he want?"

"It's complicated."

"And you think I won't understand." Corey huffed and shook his head. "Because I'm just a kid."

"No. It's not like that at all. *I* don't even understand it, really." Carin sighed and shifted in the desk, turning toward him. She'd made a mess of things, and now, looking back on it all, she had a hard time understanding just how she'd allowed it all to happen. At the time, Phillip had seemed genuinely concerned—even kind-hearted. She'd ignored every red flag...each niggle of doubt that had surfaced along the way, until it was too late. Now, everything seemed so clear, but it no longer mattered. The damage was done.

"It's a long story, Corey, but Phillip hurt my brother. I think he...I mean, I *know* he bought alcohol for my brother, and it led to other things...bad things. I didn't know that until later, kind of like putting the pieces of a puzzle together. But when I learned the truth, and confronted him about it, it made him mad. And I guess that's why he hurt me—wants to still hurt me."

"How did you find out?"

"I found a journal my brother kept...later on, after—well, just after."

"How old was your brother?"

"Only seventeen. He was about to start his senior year of high school."

"Wow." Corey let out a low whistle. "Jake would have my hide, for sure, if he ever caught me with beer or anything like that."

"Be glad for that, Corey. I know you think Jake's tough on you, but it's just because he cares so much and pays attention. Being a pastor, working with kids, he knows all the dangers that are out there...and he worries, too."

"I know. Maybe not here"—Corey tapped a finger against the side of his head—"but here." He pressed a splayed palm to his chest, right over his heart. "It still bugs the heck out of me sometimes, though. Everyone else gets away with stuff, but me...no way. I think Jake's part hawk."

"Maybe so." Carin laughed as she placed her elbow on the desk top and rested her chin on the upturned palm of her hand. "How's the newspaper coming this week?"

"Good. Amy did most of the work...since I have football practice and all."

"The two of you work pretty well together, and I'm glad because I guess I *did* pile a lot on your plate."

"Why?"

"You remind me of Cameron, before...." She lowered her gaze, the truth stirring a wave of emotions...and memories.

"He died, didn't he?"

"Yes, he did." She nodded sharply, her throat suddenly tight. "I see something in you, Corey, something that tugs on my heart."

"What?"

"A smart kid who's struggling to figure out how life works."

"I don't feel smart anymore." Corey frowned. "It used to be so easy—school. I didn't even have to think much. But now, it's really hard to care. I mean, nothing is for sure, right? I can walk outside and get hit by a mail truck or struck by lightning and that's it—game over. So why bother?"

"Because there are two sides to every coin, and what if nothing bad happens and you're here for the long haul? What are you going to do with your life—just sit around and wait for the next tragedy?"

"That's what Jake says. He's Mr. Sunshine, for sure. And I can't figure out why. I've pretty much ruined his life."

"Doesn't look that way from my corner."

"No?"

"No."

There was a slight pause as Corey considered her words. Then he nodded slightly and continued. "Jake said your mom died, too."

Carin sucked in a breath. "That's right."

"So you get it, don't you?"

"Uh-huh." She knew exactly what he meant.

"The kids here, most of them don't. They look at me like I have some kind of disease. Some ask stupid questions, and the rest avoid talking about my parents—or the fact that I live with Jake—altogether. Amy and Dillon are the only ones who don't make me feel...weird. At least not *that* kind of weird."

"There'll be others who'll understand, the older you get. I promise."

"Yesterday...what happened...well, it brought back a lot of memories. I wish they just...wouldn't still hurt so much."

"I know what you mean." Carin twisted the mother-of-pearl ring she always wore on her right index finger—a gift handed down from her grandmother to her mom, and then to her at her high school graduation several years ago. "I wish I had an answer for that, but I don't. I guess it just takes time."

"I like the way you admit it when you don't know the

answer to something. Some people—well, they act like they know everything." Corey rolled his eyes. "No one knows everything, not even Jake."

"You're right." Carin studied Corey's expressive blue eyes, the same shade as Jake's, and the dark waves of hair that were a mirror of Jake's, as well. He fidgeted, running his finger along a ridge someone had carved into the surface of the desk top with a pen. "Jake said you had nightmares after we found Scooter."

"Not too bad. They still come every once in a while, but I can deal with it." Corey shrugged. "Jake likes you—a lot. I can tell by the way he looks at you, kind of dewy-eyed."

"Dewy-eyed." Carin laughed. "That's so—"

"Corny, I know."

"I was going to say sweet. That's so sweet."

"Whatever. At first, it made me mad—and kind of scared, if you really want to know the truth. Because I thought, well, that you'd be like Rachelle. She wanted Jake to send me to a foster home." He sucked a breath, shook his head. "She hated me. Talk about having nightmares."

"I know. Jake told me."

"He did?" Cory's eyes widened. "I'm glad he didn't...send me away, I mean."

"Me, too." Carin stretched a hand across the desk to brush the hair from his eyes. "He never would, no matter how hard you try to make him. You don't need to worry about that. It's a waste of energy."

Corey held her gaze. "You're not like her...like Rachelle. Not at all."

"Hmmm..." Carin's hand slipped to his cheek for the slightest moment before she drew back. "Thanks."

"I just wanted to tell you that. I needed to—" He turned as footsteps echoed down the hall. "I'll bet that's Jake."

Carin glanced at the clock above the white board. "Five-fifteen. I'll bet your right."

Jake rounded the corner and strode through the doorway. "Hey, Corey."

"Hey back."

"Hi, Carin." He leaned against the doorjamb as his gaze locked with hers. She imagined he saw the dark circles that shadowed her eyes. She'd done her best to conceal them beneath a layer of makeup that morning but had failed miserably. "You doing OK?"

"Yeah." She unfolded herself from the desk, went to him, and sighed as he pulled her in. The soft fabric of his polo shirt, the clean scent of aftershave, comforted. "And you?"

He kissed the top of her head. "A little road weary, but good. I've been at meetings all day, and then made a quick trip to the hospital to visit with Mrs. Landers after she came out of surgery."

"How is she?"

"Healing just fine. She said to thank you for the books you sent over. She'll have plenty of time to read while she's recovering."

"Good. I'm glad she liked them."

"I missed lunch." Jake patted his belly and turned to Corey. "You hungry?"

"You know I am."

"How about some Chinese from Ming Tree? You haven't made silly faces at the koi fish for a while. I bet they miss you."

"Probably." Corey slipped from the desk and grabbed his equipment bag. "But I only want to go if Miss O'Malley comes, too."

"That works," Jake said. "Because I went to check on Scooter, and the vet said he'll be well enough to come home tonight."

"Really?" Corey gave a fist pump.

"Yes, really." Jake smiled. "So gather your stuff and let's go."

"On the way to dinner can we stop at Amy's house to drop off her homework?"

"Homework?" Jake pressed a hand to Corey's forehead. "Who are you, and where is my brother?"

⧽⧼

Jake watched the two of them—Corey and Carin—and realized that something in Corey had changed. It was a subtle change, granted, but a change all the same. What had he missed? Corey listened and laughed—actually laughed—over a silly joke Carin shared. Imagine that.

Once Rachelle snubbed him, Corey wouldn't give her the time of day. It got to the point, in fact, that if Jake was with one it meant not being with the other, or enduring a litany of jabs passed back and forth until he could no longer stand it.

Again, he tried not to compare but couldn't seem to help himself.

After dinner, they picked up Scooter from the vet and then drove to Carin's house. Corey sat on the living room floor, cuddling the cat like a baby. He refused to let go.

"I still wish you'd file a restraining order," Jake said to Carin. "Then if anything else happens, at least they'll have some kind of record."

"I went yesterday morning." Carin drew a sip of coffee.

"Why didn't you tell me?" Jake took the coffee mug from her hand, set it on the kitchen table, and then drew her close. He pressed his lips to the crown of her hair, inhaled the sweet scent of sandalwood before dipping lower, to her cheek, and then finally her mouth. He tasted, savored, then drew back. "I would have gone with you."

"I needed to do it alone. I'm putting an end to Phillip's assault, Jake." She clung to him, her heart thumping against his chest. "I'm tired of feeling afraid, of holding onto the hurt. I just don't want to hurt anymore."

"I'm glad." He sighed as his insides struggled to make sense of it all. "Because I care about you, Carin. I'm beginning to…fall in love with you. But even more than that, Corey cares about you, too. God has used you to ignite a change in him greater than any I imagined in my prayers. You've given him—and me—hope again."

# 16

Carin thought she might not be able to find it, but after only one wrong turn and a bit of backtracking she located the gravel road that led to the gigantic oak—Jake's wisdom tree.

She felt a bit like an intruder as she took a blanket from her car and strode toward the tree, but she needed a quiet place to think—to sort everything out—and this was the first place that came to mind.

She spread the blanket beneath the tree and settled in, leaning her back against the sturdy trunk to gaze over the valley below. Clouds gathered like lamb's wool and the breeze nipped, hinting that autumn was inching toward winter. A hawk circled overhead, reminding her of Corey's comment.

*I think Jake's part hawk.*

Carin sighed. From here, everything seemed so peaceful and serene. Why couldn't life really be that way? The scent of decaying leaves, earthy and musty, filled her nose. The ground was damp, and moss grew all around the base of the trunk, like a soft layer of tiny pillows. Above her, a crimson cardinal flitted about the oak's web of branches, adding a splash of color. Carin wondered if it was the same bird she and Jake had seen the last time she was here.

She reached into the tote she'd brought, found the Bible Jake had given her and flipped it open to Psalms. The book had so many great messages, and she needed to hear them now. Maybe, somewhere in the words, she'd find an answer…and a path.

She'd reported the history of Phillip's actions to the police and secured a restraining order against him, but that wasn't the end of things, she knew. She still had Cameron's journal—

though her dad didn't know it existed. She knew she had to tell him about it—should have done so immediately—and now the omission weighed heavily, even though her reasons for withholding the truth seemed valid at the time.

Things were so mixed up, and a lack of sleep made it even harder to focus. Almost a week had passed since the break in, and though the police report was filed, she still jumped at the slightest night creak. Scooter, thank goodness, was healing nicely, but the vet said he'd probably always walk with a limp. Carin grew misty-eyed at the way he mewled as she filled his food dish, and how he tried to wind figure-eight's around her ankles, so happy to see her when she came home from work. The realization of how close she'd come to losing him made her tremble.

She thought of Jake—the strength of him and his kind and giving heart. He'd found Scooter and had whisked him to the vet quickly enough to save the cat's life. He knew she loved Scooter, and that, clearly, was all that mattered to him. Jake had befriended her—fallen in love with her—and all she'd given him was a bushel full of trouble and a slew of unanswered questions. Where was the fairness in that?

Carin loved him, too. She knew it with every fiber of her being. But she didn't deserve him. That, she also knew. Not if something didn't change, and quick. The flash of hurt in his eyes when she refused to share with him told the story. She couldn't hurt him, not any more than she already had. She'd pray for the right words and then tell him about Phillip—the whole story…somehow.

అ∽ఓ

Jake saw the sedan as soon as he crested the hill and was thankful for his good instincts. Carin was seated beneath the tree, her legs stretched along a blanket and her head dipped toward a book. He recognized the navy cover and knew it was the Bible he'd given her. Carin didn't see him, and he hadn't alerted her by sound either, since he'd parked the Jeep at the base of the drive and hiked up.

He struggled between staying and going. She obviously needed time to be alone, to sort out whatever was going through that pretty little head of hers. But he had needs, too, and what better place to talk it out than here—beneath the canopy of the wisdom tree.

Maybe his hesitation came in the fact that he knew whatever she was harboring had to be pretty serious, or she would have shared it already. And he also sensed that whatever it was might change things between them, maybe things that were too big to fix. And then what? Could he walk away with his heart shattered?

He shook his head as he crossed the pasture, already knowing the answer. He loved Carin, and nothing she told him would change that. Nothing.

A twig snapped beneath his tennis shoe, and Carin lifted her head. Her gaze locked with his, and for a moment confusion held the reins. But then understanding took over, and she set down the Bible.

"Jake, you startled me."

"Sorry. I didn't want to disturb you. You looked so...engrossed."

"Psalms usually does that to me." She reached into her tote, pulled out a bottle of water. "Take this. You look...hot."

He laughed, remembering the first time they met. "Thanks."

"How did you know I was here?"

"I didn't, for sure. I just had a hunch." He settled on the blanket beside her and leaned back against the tree. "I stopped by school to surprise you with lunch, but Hailey said you took a personal day. So I checked your house, saw your car was gone, and just figured..." He shrugged. "I don't know."

"You could have just called."

"Nah...too easy."

Carin laughed. "So, where's the lunch?"

"Here." He placed a bag on the blanket. "I know how you like grilled chicken salad, so I stopped by that place in town that you mentioned and got you one. I hope I asked for the right type of dressing."

"Oh, Jake, that's so...sweet."

"Sweet's my middle name—unless Corey's mad at me, then I'm sure he comes up with something else altogether."

Again, Carin laughed. "Share with me?"

"No thanks." He shook his head and loosened the cap on the bottle of water. "No rabbit food for me. I'll stick to burgers."

"But you didn't bring a burger."

"I ate it in the car on the way here." He rubbed his belly. "It's a job requirement. Pastors need to be experts at eating on the run. We do it *a lot*."

"I see." Carin opened the white paper bag, drew out a foil tin with a cardboard cover. "This smells good."

"Hope it tastes good, too."

She tore open a package of ranch dressing, dumped half on the salad, and put the rest back in the bag. "I'm sorry you missed me at work."

"But I found you here."

"Even better." She slipped a forkful of salad into her mouth, chewed, swallowed. "Was my class behaving for the substitute?"

"You don't want to know."

"*Arghh*." She speared a piece of chicken. "No more personal days for me."

Jake laughed. "I can see the slew of writing assignments now."

"Jake?" Carin balanced the salad on her lap as she reached for a bottle of water. "I'm glad you came here. I...want to talk to you."

"I was hoping you would."

"There's so much to say. I don't know where to start."

"The beginning's a good place."

"Maybe." She sighed. "I know I've been elusive...sharing things with you. I don't mean to be, truly. It's just...the deeper I get, the harder it is to dig myself out."

"I know what you mean." He slipped in beside her and settled his back against the trunk of the tree. "I've been there, too."

"Did you ever have something that hurt so much, made you so angry, that you knew you had to purge yourself of it, but you just couldn't seem to let go?"

"I've lost my parents, Carin. My fiancée made me choose…" He snatched a tomato from her salad and popped it into his mouth. "People think because I'm a pastor, that I have some super-human ability to deflect the basic human emotions—fear, hurt, anger, resentment—but I don't. I feel the same as they do…as you do."

"But you seem different, somehow—stronger."

"I think sometimes God pulls you to the very depths of the ocean before he helps you make that climb to the summit. I've been there, Carin, and through it I learned to embrace the power of prayer. It's the only way."

"I've tried…truly I have. God just doesn't seem to be listening."

"Oh, He is. He just works in His own time."

"How can I trust that, Jake? I want to, but I feel like I'm caught on a suspension bridge, and the wind is gusting. I'm going to fall."

"God will catch you." Jake reached for the Bible. "Keep reading this. It's full of His promises."

"I have to make peace with it—with what happened to Cameron—the best I can. It's time, Jake."

"I understand."

"I spoke to my dad last night. He's coming for a visit this weekend. I'd like you to meet him."

"I'd like that, too."

Jake opened the Bible to one of the pages he'd color coded with a sticky strip, and began to read.

"'Blessed is the man who trusts in the Lord, whose confidence is in Him. He will be like a tree planted by the water, that sends out its roots by the stream. It does not fear when heat comes; its leaves are always green. It has no worries in a year of drought and never fails to bear fruit.'"

"That's beautiful," Carin murmured. "What is it?"

"From the book of Jeremiah, chapter 17. It's one of my favorites."

"You have a lot of favorites, don't you?"

"Uh-huh."

"Read me another passage. Your voice...it calms me."

He flipped through the pages. "What would you like to hear?"

"Another of your favorites."

He settled on Psalms and read until Carin got her fill of salad. Then he paused to help her gather the empty carton back into the bag.

"Jake?" She glanced up at him as their fingers touched.

"I'm here, Carin."

"I have some things I need to tell you." She caught her lower lip between her teeth, let it go, and rested her hands in her lap. "Things I *want* to share with you about Phillip...and me."

"I'm listening."

"OK. I—"

His phone rang and he groaned as he drew it from his pocket and checked the caller ID. He lifted his gaze to her. "I'm sorry. I have to take this."

❧❦

She waited. He spoke only a few words, listened a length of time, and then disconnected, his mouth drawn, eyes dark with concern. "I'm sorry, Carin. I have to go. Pastor Julian...he just passed away."

"Oh, Jake. I'm so sorry." Tears blurred her vision, and her throat tightened with grief. "Do you want me to come?"

"No." He shook his head. "You stay here. I'll call you when I can—later." He rocked to his feet and bent to kiss her. "I'm sorry...I want to hear what you have to say, truly I do."

"I know. But it can wait. Pastor Julian..."

Jake's breath hitched and tears filled his eyes. The pastor...the man...clamped a fist to his mouth to stifle a sob, and it broke her. She drew him in, pressing her cheek to his T-shirt. His heart thumped beneath the fabric, matching the cadence of hers.

"I have to go." He smoothed her hair, stroked the tension from her shoulders. "If I'm unable to get to the school before Corey finishes practice, can you pick him up this afternoon?"

"Of course. I'll take care of it. Don't worry, Jake." She smoothed a hand to his cheek, felt the shadow of stubble. "Don't worry about anything."

# 17

"You can challenge me if you want," Carin cautioned. "But I really think you'll be sorry."

"That's not a word." Corey reached for a handful of popcorn from the bowl Carin set on the table. He tossed a kernel into his mouth as he studied the Scrabble board. Nearly every space was filled, just a turn or two's worth of tiles remaining in the red-velvet pouch set to the side of the kitchen table. "At least not the way you have it spelled."

"Are you going to argue with your English teacher?" Carin gathered a handful of popcorn. The aroma of butter clung to the air, making her stomach grumble. She wondered if Jake was eating on the run again as he planned Pastor Julian's memorial. The elderly man had no family, and Jake loved him like a father. Carin tamped a wave of sadness and focused on the game. "Of course *testatrix* is a word."

"Yeah—it was one of the vocabulary words you assigned in English class. But you've spelled it wrong here. There should be an A between the T's—not an E." Corey glanced at his tiles, then the board, and Carin knew he was carefully debating his next move. "I'm going to challenge. We need a dictionary."

"Are you sure you want to do that?" Carin grabbed another fistful of popcorn. "You'll lose a turn, you know."

"Or *you'll* lose a turn, which is what I'm hoping for." Corey challenged her with his gaze. "I think you're bluffing, and I can still win this game."

"With a miracle, maybe." Carin enjoyed this bit of smack-talk. She was pleased to find Corey could hold his own. She'd bluffed him on purpose, hoping he'd rise to the challenge.

And he had. "There's a dictionary on the bookshelf in the living room. Grab it while I pour some iced tea."

Corey retreated into the living room and returned a moment later flipping through the pages of her dictionary. She knew the very moment he found the word; his tennis shoes slapped the wood floor as he commenced to victory dance. "I was right!" A grin threatened to split his face wide open. "Take your tiles off the board, Miss O'Malley."

She removed the tiles, one by one. "You *have* been paying attention in class."

"Yes, I have." He took the glass of tea she offered. "Check the score. You have to deduct those points."

"Ouch, but OK." She took a pen, recalculated their scores. "Now, tell me what it means—*testatrix*."

Corey scratched the side of his head, squinting. The gesture reminded her of Cameron, and a slight pang zinged her heart. "It's someone who's made a will."

"Be more specific." She tapped the table with the pen. "I taught you better than that."

"It's a woman!" Corey shouted, slipping back into his chair. "Yes, a testatrix is a woman who's made a will."

"Very good, Corey." Carin grinned at him before she drew a sip of tea. "Now, I guess you'd better take your turn, finish this out so you can brag to all your friends about how you beat your English teacher, of all people, at Scrabble."

"Oh, I wouldn't do that." He shook his head. "Well, maybe just to Dillon...and Amy. And of course I'd have to tell Jake, too."

"Of course." Carin laughed. "But you have to win, first."

"Oh, yeah."

"And the timer's ticking." She flipped the pint-sized hourglass and set it back on the table. "So you'd better get on it quick."

"OK. Right." He rearranged the tiles on his rack.

"And one more thing...when we're not at school you can call me Carin, if you'd like."

"Cool." Corey glanced up, caught her gaze. "I'd like that."

❧❦

Jake pushed the glider on Carin's front porch into motion and drew her close.

"I love the sound of the rain." She rested her head against his chest and sighed. "Especially rain like this—light and melodic, almost like a sweet symphony."

Jake wrapped an arm around her shoulders. Voices from the TV drifted through an open window, and he knew Corey was curled up on Carin's couch, jotting notes in his journal. "You smell like buttered popcorn."

"From our Scrabble game. I made a bowl, and Corey and I devoured it."

"Hmm…" Jake kissed her. "Tasty, too."

She laughed, pressed a hand to his chest, and his heartbeat kicked up a notch. He wondered if she could feel it through the cotton fabric of his polo shirt. "Are you holding up OK?"

"I'm good." He sighed. "But it *has* been a lot lately."

"I know. And I feel like a lot of it is…my fault."

"Stop thinking that way." Jake leaned back in the glider, listened to the dance of rain in the gutters, and thought maybe he knew what Carin meant when she called it a sweet symphony. "Corey told me he beat you at Scrabble."

"I'll bet he did."

"He's on cloud nine. Who knew what a little victory could do?"

"Glad to sacrifice my ego to the greater good."

"He's writing in his journal now, probably documenting the whole event." Jake rubbed a hand over the stubble that covered his chin. "It's about time he writes about someone besides me."

"He wrote about your parents…just this week."

"He did?" The glider paused. "Is he…OK?"

"Yeah." She nodded as the rain sluiced over the porch awning. "He got it off his chest, let go of some of the hurt. It will be easier to talk about...to write about...from this point on."

"He rarely puts that journal down now."

"I've noticed."

"How did you know...that writing would help him so much?"

"I didn't."

"But then, why?"

"Selfish reasons, I guess. To give me insight into what he's thinking...and feeling." She slipped away from him, gazed out over the rain-drenched woods as drops continued to patter the porch overhang. "I was thinking of Cameron, and how he kept a journal. But I didn't know—didn't pay much attention—until after he was gone."

"What do you mean?"

"It's what I meant to tell you this afternoon, before you got that phone call, before Pastor Julian..."

"Tell me now," Jake coaxed. "I'm listening."

Carin waited while Jake nudged the glider into motion once again. "It was hard after my mom died, to keep it all together. My dad kind of disappeared into himself—the grief overwhelmed him, I guess. He's always worked a lot of hours, but after Mom was gone, I don't know, it became so much more excessive. Cameron was left alone a lot, and he was only sixteen when Mom died. He was going through a difficult time anyway, and losing Mom, well, it just made it that much harder. I tried to talk to him, but I was busy helping Dad, and living half-an-hour away. I didn't get home to him as often as I should have."

"But the journal?"

"I found it in his room...after." Carin brushed her palms back and forth over the thighs of her jeans, then clasped her hands and settled them in her lap. "I was going through his things, trying to donate what I could and box up the rest. The journal was tucked beneath his mattress, and I felt like an intruder as I read through the passages. What would he think if he was there to see me?"

"Maybe he left it for a reason. Maybe he wanted you to find it."

"Maybe."

"Can you share what he wrote?"

Carin nodded stiffly. "He wrote about all kinds of things...things he might have shared with me, if I'd taken the time to listen. But I didn't, and by the time I found his journal it was too late." She turned to face him, tears shimmering in her eyes like the raindrops that splattered around them. "He was hurting so much, and I didn't know. I didn't listen—I didn't see. But I should have."

Jake reached for her hand. "You were grieving, too, Carin."

"But I was older. I should have protected him. I should have been there for him." The tears spilled over. "Cameron *needed* me, Jake. And I let him down."

"You did what you could with what you had to give at the time. You're only human, after all."

"Would you say the same if it were Corey?" She stood, paced. "Could you live with yourself, knowing you could have—should have—done more?"

"I don't know. If you hadn't come along to help, to see what I couldn't..." He lowered his voice, let the words—and the thought—fade away. "But what I *do* know is that the should-have's will destroy you if you let them."

She nodded, brushed a tear from her cheek. "I know that."

Jake sighed and drew her back to his side. "There's more, isn't there?"

"Yes." She nodded. "There *was* someone who listened to Cameron, someone who heard him even when I didn't."

"Who?"

"Phillip." Carin forced the word out on a sob. "I thought he was helping Cameron. I thought he genuinely cared. We were dating at the time, and he seemed to reach out, to understand just what Cameron needed. But Phillip's interest was all carefully orchestrated, just a good show in an attempt to gain a promotion at my dad's law firm. I didn't know—had no idea—until I stumbled across a series of entries near the back of Cameron's journal.

"Cameron was hurting, and I guess he mentioned something to Phillip about how hard it was at school, the way the kids stared at him like he was some kind of freak since Mom died, and how all of his friends avoided him because they didn't know what to say. His grades were slipping, and he quit the basketball team. He said no one cared—not Dad, and not me, either. He needed something...to help him cope, to get him through."

Jake rubbed her arm and gathered her closer.

"Phillip encouraged him to skip school, took him to a park where they hiked a bit before Phillip introduced him to rum and cola." She shook her head. "I remember that day, because Cameron was late getting home, and he seemed a bit off...really quiet. When I asked him about it he gave some lame answer. I was engrossed in reports for my dad, so I didn't question him further, and I should have."

"There's another ugly should-have."

Carin set the glider into motion, leaned into Jake again. "It happened with greater and greater frequency over the next several months, and then one night Cameron got arrested for vandalism at the high school. Phillip went with me to bail him out, and I thought Phillip was helping me—helping Cameron. But all he was doing was masking the truth."

"What happened after the arrest?"

"Cameron got suspended. He spent his days at the alternative school, in a cubicle, working alone. He fell into a deeper depression and sulked all the time. The arrest—and my dad's anger over it—put a strain on all of us. Cameron wasn't thinking straight, Jake. He was a different kid—messed up bad, and over the following weeks, he and Phillip only drew closer. I guess Phillip assumed if my dad thought he was helping Cameron, it would give him a leg up toward the promotion. He was pushing me, too, for more than a little dating. He said he wanted to...get married."

"But you still didn't know about the alcohol?"

"No. Phillip had his guard up all the time, though. But when I questioned him, he just said he was working hard toward a promotion, and the stress was getting to him. He started pressuring me more, but I refused to consider marriage. I think I knew, in the back of my mind, that he wasn't ready to settle down. And I was right."

"And Cameron...what happened to him?"

"He died in his sleep, two days after his seventeenth birthday...when he mixed alcohol with a handful of my dad's sedatives."

# 18

Carin gazed over the pond at the senior center. A cool breeze made rivulets of water dance across the surface as the weeping willows swayed. Clouds gathered overhead, like a ball of gray wool that seemed to unravel with each passing moment. Soon the sky would open up and cry for Pastor Julian, and for all the others loved and lost.

Carin retrained her gaze, settling on Jake, who stood at the head of the group that had gathered near the gazebo. His voice soothed as he gave the eulogy in Pastor Julian's honor.

"Pastor Julian brought humor and wisdom to my life, and to the lives of so many. He was the kind of man I hope to be. He'll be greatly missed."

Carin brushed tears from her cheeks as she glanced at Lilly, bundled beneath a quilt in the wheelchair beside her. The woman's expression was faraway, her gaze set on the shimmering water, and Carin wondered if she was thinking of the husband and daughter she'd lost so many years ago and the granddaughter who seldom found the time to come and see her.

Jake finished speaking and closed his Bible. "Thank you all for coming today and for sharing this special glimpse into Raymond Julian's life. If you'd like to join us, there's coffee and finger foods in the community room."

"I'm starving." Corey's voice broke through Carin's thoughts. He tugged the collar of his dress shirt and blew a tuft of hair from his eyes. "I'm going to head inside to grab a doughnut."

"OK. Jake and I will be there soon." She knew how hard this was for him—first his parents, then Scooter's close call, and now Pastor Julian—so much loss. It seemed to never end.

"Thanks." He turned from her and started across the grass. "I'll save you a doughnut."

"Where's he headed?" Jake rounded the gazebo, gathering his coat at the seam. The wind kicked up, and the chill was uncharacteristically sharp for an early-November, East Tennessee morning.

"Where do you think?" Carin grazed a hand across his stubbled cheek.

"He got wind of the pastries, right?" Jake's lips curved into the slightest grin, though his eyes were shadowed from yet another sleepless night. She knew he'd spent hours getting the eulogy just right, making sure all he wanted to say was included and that Pastor Julian was properly honored.

"And the soda, of course. I told him to go on, that we'd meet him there shortly." She stooped to adjust the blanket over Lilly's lap. "We'd better get you inside. The wind's kicking up."

"One more minute, Carin." Lilly closed her eyes and tipped her head back, sighing as the breeze lifted her thin, peppered hair and kissed her cheeks. "The wind is singing. Can you hear it?"

Carin stilled, allowing her eyes to close as Jake slipped his hand into hers. Through the trees, she heard a sweet melody. "I *do* hear it, Lilly. Oh, I do."

ॐ‑ॐ

Jake watched Carin from across the room as she prepared a plate of food for Lilly. With her tough but compassionate demeanor, it was easy to see why she was such an amazing teacher, one who left her imprint on the kids whose lives she touched. Corey sure had warmed to her after a bumpy start. She seemed to connect with him in a way no one else could.

Carin's words echoed through his memory…*Would you say the same if it were Corey?* Losing his folks was tough, no doubt about it. But Jake wondered how he'd survive losing

Corey. He quickly banished the thought. The day was gloomy enough. Just the idea of such a thing ripped his heart to shreds.

Carin came over, pushing Lilly's chair with one hand while she carried a plate of food in the other. "You holding up OK? You look so far away. Lost in another world."

"Just thinking." Jake brushed hair back from her face and nudged her aside to take the chair handles. "I'll give Miss Lilly a ride now."

"She wants to go back to her room. She has something she wants to show Corey."

"Oh?"

"That's right, Pastor Jake." Lilly's watery gray eyes settled on Jake as she craned her head for a look. The scent of spearmint wafted up, fresh and clean. It clung to Lilly's cotton slacks and sweater. "Take me there, please. And make sure your brother joins us. He's had enough of this stuffy old death to last a lifetime."

"Sure, Miss Lilly." Jake set the chair in motion. "Show me the way."

They gathered their plates of food, and Corey, and caravanned down the hall. Carin reached the room first. When she opened the door, Corey leaned over her shoulder to glance inside, his gaze sweeping over shelves of knickknacks and stuffed animals that lined the headboard of her twin-sized bed. The room was small, not meant for a crowd of four, but they managed to make the visit comfortable.

"Take a seat," Lilly urged. "It's OK to sit on the bed. It won't bite."

Corey flopped onto the patchwork quilt, bouncing the narrow bed so the springs protested beneath his weight. "What's this?" He reached for a photo album that lay on the bedside table.

"Corey, don't pry." Jake reached to take the album from his brother, but Lilly *shushed* him.

"Let the child look." Lilly nudged her chair closer to the bed, ignoring the plate of food Carin set on the dinette table.

"He can't hurt anything in here. It's just a bunch of this and that."

Corey flipped to the first page, and his eyes widened in astonishment. "Wow, get a load of their clothes. These pictures have to be, like, a gazillion years old."

"Corey—" Jake's voice was drowned by Lilly's cackles.

"Maybe not a gazillion...but at least a hundred," the elder woman agreed. "That's a sepia print of my great-great-grandfather. He emigrated here from Italy and was a butcher until the day he died."

"A butcher?"

"That's right. In the days before people could buy everything but a box of rocks at superstores, they used to get their steaks and chops from a local butcher."

"Cool. And who's this?" Corey tapped a second photo.

"My great-grandmother."

"She looks mad."

"Everyone looked mad back then. It wasn't proper to smile in photographs."

"Why?"

Lilly shrugged her frail shoulders. "I don't know. They just didn't."

Jake settled into a chair at the dinette while Carin boiled water in the microwave for a cup of tea. "You want one?" she whispered to Jake.

"Uh-huh." He leaned back, stretched his legs, and crossed his ankles as he loosened his tie and then unfastened the top button of his shirt. "This may take a while."

"Wow...did kids really dress like this?" Corey gaped. "In goofy pants—"

"Knickers." Lilly's voice carried across the small room.

"They look like total geeks."

Jake laughed. "I wonder if they'd think the same of you, with your hair all over your face and those sagging jeans."

Corey scratched his head, tossed hair from his eyes, and hitched up his pants. "I never thought of it that way." He leaned back in the bed, flipped through the rest of the album.

"Is this you, Miss Lilly?"

She leaned in for a glimpse though Jake was sure she had each photo in the album memorized. "Sure is. I was sixteen, at my high school prom." Her sigh was rattled. "It seems like just yesterday. Where does the time go?"

Corey smoothed a thumb across the photo. "Your hair is so...bushy."

"I did have a mop then, didn't I?" Lilly ran a hand through her thinning locks. "I *was* the bomb."

"You still are, Lilly." Jake stirred sugar into the cup of tea Carin handed him. He winked at her as she slipped into the second chair at the dinette.

"Corey, see that small plastic box on the top shelf of the bookcase?" Lilly pointed one arthritic finger. "Get it down for me, please."

"What's in it?" Corey scrambled to his knees on the bed and gathered the box. "Oh, wow! Is this for real, Miss Lilly?"

"Yes, sir...a genuine autographed home-run ball from Babe Ruth himself."

"But...how?" Corey turned the box left and right, inspecting each stitch in the scuffed leather, every letter of the inscription.

"My daddy caught that during a season opener. He and his buddy skipped school—played hooky and headed to the ball park instead. My daddy had the fever for baseball, and he sure wasn't going to miss a chance to see Babe Ruth in action."

"It's...amazing."

"It's yours now."

"What?" The bed rocked beneath Corey's weight. "No way!"

"Take it home with you; keep it, son." Lilly nodded. "I'll rest better knowing it's with someone who'll cherish it the way I have, the way my daddy did, too."

"Oh, I will, Miss Lilly. For sure. Thank you." Corey pressed the case to his chest, protecting the ball with both hands. "Jake, can I use your cell phone? I've gotta call Dillon and tell him about this!"

"Reception's better in the hall." Jake handed Corey the phone as he slipped from the bed. "We'll be here when you're done."

# 19

"Do you want me to go with you?" Jake asked as he gathered Carin close on his front porch.

"No." Carin shook her head and pressed her face to his chest, smoothing his T-shirt. She felt the slow, steady beat of his heart through the thin fabric and sighed. The rain had moved out, leaving behind cool air and a crisp, clean scent of rain-washed earth. The trees were bare, their branches naked beneath a cloud-veiled sun. "I have to talk to Dad alone, work through things with him on my own. There's no moving forward, Jake, unless I let go of the past."

"Will you call me if you need anything, keep me posted?" Jake slipped a strand of Carin's hair behind her ear, his eyes dark with questions.

"I promise."

"He'll be here soon?"

"Yes, at noon." She tried not to think about how tired her father had sounded last night as she spoke with him on the phone...how lost. His words echoed in her mind.

*"Maybe you're right, honey. Maybe I should hand some of the work off. Maybe it's time..."*

She'd try to convince him to do just that—after she showed him Cameron's journal and explained about Phillip. She just hoped his heart would hold up beneath the strain. She couldn't bear the thought of losing him, too.

"OK, then." Jake wrapped his arms around her, warming her with his embrace "I'll be praying for you...that all goes well."

"Thank you, Jake. I know now...the power of prayer."

❧

Jake watched her drive away, his gut a mass of tight knots. He knew she was seeking closure, understood that she needed to talk things out with her dad. Yet he couldn't shake the sense of dread that flooded him.

"You OK?" Corey asked through the screen door.

"Yeah."

"You don't look OK." Corey loped onto the porch and leaned against the rail. "You look like you did the night you told me about Mom and Dad."

Jake's head snapped up. "Really?"

"Yeah."

"I'm just…worried." Jake raked a hand through his hair and chose his words carefully. There was no point in worrying Corey, too. "She's been through so much."

"So have you." Corey's blue eyes narrowed with concern. "You love her, don't you?"

"Yes." Jake's gut tightened, and the knots multiplied tenfold. "Yes, I do."

"Well, when someone loves you and you love them, too, you should give it everything you have—not hold back. I mean, you can't be afraid of it."

"You sound very Shakespearean, very Romeo and Juliet."

"Yeah, well, I've got this awesome English teacher who really knows her stuff. She's a drill sergeant, though—tough as nails."

Jake laughed. "Tougher than your big brother?"

"Depends on the day." He nudged the toe of his tennis shoe against the porch rail, fidgeting. "Seriously, though…maybe you should pray about it." Corey shook his bangs from his eyes. "Ask for a little direction. That's what you always tell me, isn't it?"

Jake studied his brother, noting the clear blue of his eyes, the way he tilted his head to the side while he was thinking, in the same manner as their mother. His advice was so simple, yet it struck a chord in Jake. "You're right."

"Oh, did you see my "fortune" from the last time we ate at Ming Tree?" Corey handed Jake a small slip of paper. "Since when do they hand out Bible verses instead of fortunes?"

Jake's heart caught as he read the verse...*The Lord is good, a refuge in times of trouble. He cares for those who trust in Him.* "Oh, Corey..."

"What?"

"You're right. We need to pray."

☙⚬❧

"Daddy, I have something to show you." Carin took the journal from a cabinet beneath the bookshelf in her living room. "I found this in Cameron's room...after he died."

"What is it, honey?"

"A journal...Cameron's journal." She gathered Scooter into her arms and settled on the couch beside her father. Scooter purred and nudged the journal with his snout.

Her dad glanced at the cloth-covered book. Cameron had doodled over the cover, adding his own artwork. The jagged designs foreshadowed the entries inside. "I didn't know he kept a journal."

"I didn't, either...until I found it tucked beneath his mattress." She swallowed hard. "I should have shown it to you right away. I was wrong to keep it from you. I thought I was doing the right thing...because I didn't want to hurt you. But now things are out of hand. You'll understand when you read it." She nodded. "I hope you can forgive me, Dad."

His gaze held hers for the longest time. "This is going to change my life, isn't it?"

"Yes. But I think you should read it. You *have* to read it."

"Now? Here?"

"Yes, Daddy. I'll sit with you."

He took a pair of reading glasses from his shirt pocket and perched them on his nose before opening the journal to the first entry. He drew a single, deep sigh and began to read. Carin had memorized the entries, and she knew by the hitch in his voice just when he skimmed the most difficult words.

Tears streamed down his face as he continued, and his hiccoughs caused Carin's belly to lurch. She leaned back, raking a hand through her curls and imagining Cameron's soft-spoken voice, the lost look in his eyes during his final days. If only she had known...if only she'd paid closer attention. She held Scooter closer and stroked the scruff of his neck.

"Oh, Carin..." Her father's voice brought her back. "All this time...I had no idea."

"How could you? I hid it from you."

"Why?" He removed the glasses, his gaze riddled with confusion.

She felt tears well in her eyes.

"Because I love you, Daddy, and I didn't want to see you hurt anymore. I knew the words—Cameron's words—would wound you." She cleared her throat. "And I know how much you care for Phillip—that you think of him as a son."

"But you've carried the burden alone."

"No, I haven't, Dad. God's helped me...truly. I haven't carried it alone. I've leaned on God and it's changed me—in here." She clasped a hand over her heart.

"And Phillip...his motives..."

"I don't want revenge, Daddy. I just want closure. Don't you want that, too?"

"Yes. But I need time...to think about all of this, to process it, to grieve."

"I understand." She'd had months, and still the memories cut deeply. "But I think Phillip should pack his things and find another law firm...right, Dad?"

"He already has. He left last week."

"Really?"

"An investigator came to ask questions...something about a missing house key and a cat?"

"So the police did follow through. I'm relieved and glad for that."

"I'm not following you, honey."

"Never mind." Carin shook her head as a renewed sense of calm filled her. "No matter, Dad. Are you OK?"

"I will be…now, I will be."

"Can we go for a drive? There's someone I'd like you to meet."

പ്ര൶

Jake waited on the porch. As soon as the car turned in, he rushed to meet Carin and her father.

The resemblance was unmistakable…the light hair and green eyes. But her father was much taller, and he walked with an air of confidence gleaned from decades in a courtroom. His handshake, the eye contact, spoke volumes.

"I made coffee," Jake offered, his gaze joining with Carin's. "Come on inside, and I'll pour you a cup."

They gathered at the kitchen table, sharing turkey-on-wheat sandwiches and oatmeal-raisin cookies as they swapped work stories. It was a safe topic—one without painful memories. Corey tossed sidelong glances at Mr. O'Malley throughout the meal, sizing him up as he devoured his sandwich and sipped from a cold glass of milk, most likely wondering about the wife and son he'd lost—same as Jake wondered.

Somehow, amid the grief, they managed to share laughter. Jake poured a fresh round of coffee and refilled the cookie plate.

"Do you mind if Amy hangs out for a while?" Corey asked as he gathered a handful of cookies. "Her parents won't let her go to the arcade, either."

"Interesting." Jake sipped his coffee. "So I'm not the only dictator in East Ridge, huh?"

"I guess not." Corey shrugged. "But I still don't think it's fair."

"Good lesson for life." Jake leaned back in his chair. "A good chunk of it isn't fair."

"I'm going to start a page in my journal titled, *Quotes from*

*Jake*." Corey set his plate in the kitchen sink. "Maybe one day I'll get it published."

"Good..." Jake grinned. "Here's another one—youngest in the house does the dishes."

"That's not a quote."

"Oh, but it is." Carin laughed. "Jake said it, so, technically it *is* a quote."

Corey rolled his eyes and gathered the rest of the plates. "I'll bet Amy would like to play a game of Scrabble."

"I'm in." Jake glanced at Carin. "I'd like my shot at beating the English teacher."

She winked and leaned in for a kiss. "Who do you think taught me?"

Mr. O'Malley's laughter filled the room.

# Epilogue

Carin nestled in the pew between her dad and Corey as Jake approached the pulpit. Sunlight streamed through stained-glass windows that lined either side of the church, bathing the worshipers in a warm, soothing glow. The keyboard sang in cadence with Carin's heart.

God was good, and His grace had set her free.

Her dad glanced over, smiling. He looked a dozen years younger, the weight of guilt lifted from his shoulders. He'd carried it like an anchor, just as she had. The days and weeks that followed his reading of Cameron's journal had been tough. He'd cried, raged, and even made a trip to the emergency room, his chest so constricted with grief he felt certain he'd suffered a heart attack.

They'd spent hours on the phone, talking things out, until they'd both let it go...every last ounce.

And now her dad had moved to East Ridge—left Nashville, and his law practice there—for good. He was working in Knoxville, sharing pro-bono work with another attorney at the teen crisis center. He told Carin he hadn't felt so at peace in years, and she believed him.

Corey shifted in the seat, and she marveled at how far he'd come since the first day she met him—a scared and rebellious kid in her class. He'd had his hair trimmed, and his eyes shone bright and content beneath dark lashes. She noticed the way he scanned the room, searching for Amy MacGregor, who'd joined the church just before Thanksgiving. The two went together to visit Lilly each Tuesday, drinking in her stories and offering their friendship. Sometimes they took Scooter along, and even helped the recreational therapists lead games of bingo and their favorite—Scrabble. They'd used a computer to modify the game board and letter tiles, making both larger and easy to see.

The music lilted as Jake rose for the opening prayer. He turned to face the congregation, and his gaze locked with Carin's while winter sun streamed through the windows, adorning the cross on the front wall in a rainbow of colors. Love gathered in Carin's belly, and enfolded her heart like a warm scarf.

A sparkle of light caught her eye, and she glanced down at her left hand to find proof of another promise—Jake's promise of marriage. He'd proposed to her just last month, beneath the shelter of the wisdom tree, as Corey looked on. Soon, the three would become a family. Carin knew with all her heart that their unconditional love was the greatest testament to the power of God's grace and healing—and their hope for the future—together.

# WISDOM TREE

# DAILY DEVOTIONAL

I hope you enjoyed reading Wisdom Tree as much as I enjoyed writing it. Just as Jake and Carin did in the story, we all need Wisdom. Their lives were an overwhelming whirlwind filled with worry, doubt, and occasionally even regret. It was only when each took the time to ask for God's guidance—to commune with Him and seek His wisdom—that they gained a true sense of peace.

Over the years, I have learned that wisdom is the result of reflection—of experiences, feelings, and relationships that are our own personal gifts from God. No experience, whether joyful of painful, should be dismissed without quiet reflection. The question is, with our hectic lives, how do we find the time?

I believe our own personal Wisdom Tree is the answer. Jake's place was a beautiful ancient oak surrounded by meadows and a Smoky Mountain valley. My place is a back porch swing that my husband installed for my birthday. That little corner of my world is quiet and peaceful, and away from distractions. I like to curl up in the swing first thing in the morning to read, reflect, and pray before daily distractions take priority. It's become a habit—one that I'm hesitant to break.

Hopefully the devotionals herein will help you to find your Wisdom Tree. Carve out a small slice of time each day. Start with Day One and continue with a new devotional each day. By the end of the month you will have developed a habit of prayerful retreat and communion—an ongoing conversation with the Lord that will always be fruitful. Make communicating with God a priority. Find your Wisdom Tree. Give Him fifteen minutes a day. Reflect and pray and you will begin to experience peace and personal growth, and thus deeper wisdom regarding the plans the Lord has for you.

DAY One

## Dumping the Garbage

*If anyone is in Christ, he is a new creation;*
*the old has gone, the new has come!*
*(2 Corinthians 5:17)*

This morning I took my trash to the dump...a whole truck-bed full of pizza boxes and soiled paper towels and the remainder of meals prepared and shared. While I was tossing each heavy bag into the dumpster, I thought of how God takes the trash from our lives. He cleans out the stinky stuff and makes room for the good stuff. God is the Master of new creations. He wants His people to let go of the old and soiled, and to become new and clean in Him.

Yes, this is God's desire...and His plan for you.

REFLECT: Take a moment to gather your trash. Bind it and carry it to the feet of God. Leave it there, and God will make you new in Him.

PRAY: Lord, today I offer you all my worries and shortcomings that keep me from You and from attaining the peace and grace You have in store for me.

## DAY Two

### God's Closet

*You were taught, with regard to your former way of life, to put off your old self, which is being corrupted by its deceitful desires; to be made new in the attitude of your minds; and to put on the new self, created to be like God in true righteousness and holiness.*
*(Ephesians 4:22-24)*

Going shopping for new clothes is usually fun. The fabric is fresh and crisp, the styles are up-to-date, and you dream of the wonderful adventures you'll have while wearing a new outfit. But, eventually, the fabric fades, shrinks, and goes out of style.

The clothes in God's closet never go out of style. The fabric of His truth never fades, and His love never shrinks. Living with God is like putting on a new outfit each day. We are clothed in His righteousness.

REFLECT: Take a moment to search His closet to find the outfit meant for you. Thank Him for new beginnings each and every morning, and go into the world for the adventure He desires you to seek—to share His message with others.

PRAY: Lord, today I open myself to Your will. Clothe me in Your righteousness and grant me the strength and wisdom to be Your ambassador.

DAY Three

**Window Shopping**

*The Lord does not look at the things man looks at. Man looks at the*
*outward appearance, but the Lord looks at the heart.*
(1 Samuel 16:7)

We've all done it—walked down the street and glanced
into a store window, only to be captivated by the allure of the
products on display. Perhaps there's a fire-engine red toolbox
with all the latest gadgets, dinnerware with a delicate pattern,
or a sequined blouse that's sure to make you the hit of the
party. You get the idea. So you go into the store, hand over
your money, and take your treasures home. But, upon closer
inspection, you find the toolbox lacks the one gizmo you need,
the dishes crack, and the sequins come loose from their fabric.
Disappointment replaces excitement.

God looks beyond the display window and into your
heart. He knows your value, and the beauty hidden inside
you. God understands that things of the world lose their luster
and often fail to live up to expectation. But His word never
fades away, and it never fails those who seek Him.

REFLECT: Take a moment to talk to Him, then be still and
listen as He examines your heart.

PRAY: Lord, allow me to rest in the assurance that my
true worth lies in the price Christ paid to ransom my soul.
Grant me the grace not to desire things of this world, but only
to hope for a deep and lasting relationship with You. Your will
be done.

DAY Four

## Waiting at the Check-out

*Be still before the Lord and wait patiently for Him; do not fret when men succeed in their ways, when they carry out their wicked schemes. Refrain from anger and turn from wrath; do not fret—it leads only to evil. (Psalm 37: 7-8)*

You've been there…on your way to the grocery check-out line. Of course, your cart houses only the essentials, and you're in a hurry to get home to prepare dinner. Suddenly, a fellow shopper rounds the corner, her cart overflowing, and swoops into the line ahead of you. A two-minute shopping trip just multiplied five-fold, and you feel your temper simmer. You want to stomp your foot and shout, "Who do you think you are? Can't you see I'm in a hurry?"

Life does that to us sometimes. We have a plan, and things detour at the last minute. Kids get sick, dinner burns, the dog eats the homework, or we take the wrong exit from the highway. But God is always there, and He asks us to be patient and to trust Him. His ways are rock-solid, and He has already won the race for us. In His time, there are no sick kids, no burned meals or dog-slobbered papers. He knows the right exit, and He's already there, waiting for you.

REFLECT: Take time today to slow down and breathe. Remember God's timing is perfect, so perhaps there's grace within the delay.

PRAY: Lord, grant me increased patience while I find my way to You. Help me to always remember that You are with me and that Your plan and Your timing are perfect.

DAY Five

## Jumping From the High Dive

*The Lord Himself goes before you; He will never leave you nor forsake you. Do not be afraid; do not be discouraged.*
*(Deuteronomy 31:8)*

It's the last day of summer, the last day of sun-dappled water and carefree fun. Your stomach is in knots, because you're standing at the edge of the high dive, staring down into the water. Your friends wait on the pool deck, cheering for you, and you know it's now or never. Jump today, or live with the disappointment of your lack of bravery until a whole year passes and next summer arrives. Stay or go? Wait or jump?

Sometimes, life brings changes and challenges that seem insurmountable. Rest assured; God is waiting to catch you. He's there beneath the high dive with His arms open wide and a smile on His face. He whispers gentle words of encouragement. "Jump to me. I will catch you no matter how far the distance. You are safe in my embrace."

REFLECT: Take a moment to reflect on God's steadfastness. What are the challenges in your life, the fears that bind you? How can you grow to trust your Lord and Savior?

PRAY: Lord, today I surrender all my fears to You. I know you are always there, even in the midst of trial, and You will never let me go.

DAY Six

## Finding the Path

*Let the morning bring me word of your unfailing love, for I have put my trust in you. Show me the way I should go, for to you I lift up my soul.*
*(Psalm 143:8)*

While hiking several years ago, I trusted my friend when he claimed he knew the way through the mountainous back country. "Put your map away and follow me," he said. "I know a shortcut."

So, I put away the map and followed him. We hiked for several hours, and my skin was scratched and bleeding from fighting rhododendron bushes and stumbling over gnarled tree roots. Soon, I realized he was walking in circles...and I was following. I finally got up the nerve to ask the question I already knew the answer to, "We're lost, aren't we?"

God gives us a map—His word, the Bible. But sometimes the world entices us to follow alternate routes...and we decide to take the shortcut—to riches, relationships, or perhaps fame. We stumble and fall until we listen for His voice.

REFLECT: Consider all the times you've chosen to take a shortcut in life—all the times you've turned from His truth and directive in favor of ease or material gain. Seek him, and study His map—the Bible. It will take you to the places you're meant to go...safely and in *His* time.

PRAY: Lord, help me to put aside what the world beckons. Help me to turn from the songs of speed and greed, so that I may take to heart the path You have laid out for me.

DAY Seven

## Just for the Record…

*O Lord, hear my voice.*
*Let Your ears be attentive to my cry for mercy.*
*If You, O Lord, kept a record of sins, who could stand?*
*But with you there is forgiveness; therefore you are feared.*
*I wait for the Lord, my soul waits.*
*And in His word I put my hope.*
*(Psalm 130:2-5)*

Keeping a record of sins is like writing the weekly grocery list: milk—check, bread—check, revenge on my co-worker for that insensitive comment—check and double check. We like lists; they give us a sense of accomplishment. But checking off a list of sins does not satisfy us like completing chores or filling our bellies with food. No, a record of sins just serves to keep those transgressions alive in our hearts and minds, weighing us down in our daily walk.

God does not keep a list of our sins. When we seek forgiveness, He takes our harsh words, our impatience, our gossip and dark thoughts and casts them into the wind. If He does this for us, is it so difficult for us to follow His example and do the same for our family members, our neighbors and co-workers…even our enemies and ourselves?

REFLECT: Consider your transgressions and then ask God to blot them out. Instead, of holding in your heart that list of sins already forgiven, seek to fill your heart with His word and His wisdom.

PRAY: Lord, I am truly sorry for failing to live according

to Your word and for choosing, instead, to wrong. I ask You to forgive my sins and to grant me the grace I need to let go of the guilt, to leave the past in the past, and not to sin again.

DAY Eight

## Roll Call

*Fear not, for I have redeemed you; I have summoned you by name; you are mine. I will be with you; and when you pass through the rivers, they will not sweep over you. When you walk through the fire, you will not be burned; the flames will not set you ablaze. For I am the Lord, your God, the Holy one of Israel, your Savior.*
*(Isaiah 43:1-3)*

The beginning of the school year always presents a challenge for me—to learn the name of each new student as quickly as possible. The task seems to get more and more difficult as I age. There are thousands of students on the attendance roll tucked within my heart. Over the decades, each child has been entrusted to me, his or her life and learning placed into my hands. I don't want to fail them; each is special and unique.

God calls our name—each and every one of us. Yet the task is never difficult for Him; He doesn't age or grow weary, and He never fails His children. We are safe in His arms, for the Bible tells us that God knows every detail of our lives, down to the exact number of hairs on our head. It's easy to forget how unique and special we are to Him. When the storms of life rage, we may believe He has forgotten our name. But God has us safely in His embrace, and He knows what troubles us. Seek Him and listen, and you will hear Him call your name.

REFLECT: Think of those times in your life when you have felt completely overwhelmed. In hindsight, were those situations as debilitating as you had first thought?

PRAY: Lord, help me to hear You calling my name, calling me into Your presence so that I may be at peace in all situations.

DAY Nine

## A Light in the Storm

*Your word is a lamp to my feet and a light to my path.*
*(Psalm 119:105)*

A thunderstorm raged one spring night. It knocked out our electricity and woke my daughter from a sound sleep. She cried out, scared in the darkness. I went to her, carrying a flashlight. The beam calmed her, and in the wash of light, she was able to once again succumb to the peace of sleep.

God is our beam of light in the storm. His word is the flashlight that guides us when thunder rages and the wind howls. He takes us to high ground when the floods threaten to sweep us away. God's light never dims; His batteries never need recharging.

REFLECT: Pause for a moment to rejoice in His light, and to thank Him for ushering us into the halo.

PRAY: Lord, I want to share in Your light. Help me to listen and to be cognizant of the opportunities You present so that I may go into the world and become a beacon for You.

DAY Ten

**Why Me, Lord?**

*We also rejoice in our sufferings; because we know that suffering produces perseverance; perseverance, character; and character, hope. And hope does not disappoint us, because God poured out His love into our hearts by the Holy Spirit, whom He has given us.*
*(Romans 5:3-5)*

Traffic jams, coffee spills, the receiving end of an irate customer's tirade. Or worse yet: job loss, debilitating illness, the death of a loved one. We've all been there, and we've all asked, "Why me?"

God doesn't want you to suffer. But He does want you to learn to lean on Him and to trust Him at all times and in all situations—not just when it's easy. He knows the plan He has for you…to bring you joy and peace.

When the things of this world fade away, He will still be here for you. Trust in Him, and trust in His word…shared to bring you comfort and peace. Why you? Because God loves you enough to call you by name. He pours out His love to you and gives you hope. Share that love, and when you hear someone ask, "Why me?"—tell them.

REFLECT: Take a moment to ponder Christ's crucifixion—the Savior, the perfect Sacrifice…a completely innocent Person made to suffer and die for the transgressions of others. Life sometimes does not seem fair, but beyond the Crucifixion was the Resurrection. Beyond all tribulation comes triumph.

PRAY: Lord, when trials come, help me to remain

steadfast in my faith. Help me to accept Your gift of sacrifice and to remain enfolded in Your grace and peace, no matter what the circumstance.

DAY Eleven

## My Invisible Friend

*Have I not commanded you? Be strong and courageous. Do not be terrified; do not be discouraged, for the Lord your God will be with you wherever you go.*
*(Joshua 1:9)*

Most children have a special friend—and sometimes that friend is invisible. Some say this friend is "imaginary." Well, God is invisible, but He's certainly not imaginary. At one time or another, we have all been immersed in situations that strike fear at our very core. The first day at a new job, a move to a new and unfamiliar place, standing in front of a crowd to speak, or waiting in the doctor's office for test results. But we are not alone. God is there beside us, with His arms wrapped lovingly around us as He surrounds us with the comfort and peace only He can provide. So, draw a breath and listen for His voice…feel His embrace.

REFLECT: Take time today to thank God for standing beside you and surrounding you with the grace only He can give. He is there always, to comfort and lead you. Ask Him to show you the way you should go, and do not be afraid to follow Him. Search His word, and learn of His boundless strength and power, provided for especially you.

PRAY: Lord, help me to trust You in all situations and at all times. You, Lord, are the almighty Author, and You know the way You will lead me, to bring peace and hope. Help me to listen for Your voice.

DAY Twelve

## In God We Trust

*Godliness with contentment is great gain. For, we brought nothing into the world, and we can take nothing out of it. But if we have food and clothing, we will be content with that. People who want to get rich fall into temptation and a trap and into many foolish and harmful desires that plunge men into ruin and destruction. For the love of money is a root of all kinds of evil. Some people, eager for money, have wandered from the faith and pierced themselves with many griefs.*
*(1 Timothy 6:6-10)*

"In God we trust" is printed on money, but how can money—an inanimate object—trust in God? Well, it falls to us—the users of money—to put that trust into action. Will we buy the newest technology gadget, or support mission work that spreads the love of God? How do you spend your dollars? Do you trust God to fulfill your needs...or do you place that trust in yourself, thinking you know what you need better than God does? And, how much is enough when it comes to worldly possessions?

REFLECT: Ask God what He would like you to do to further His kingdom. Listen for His guidance. Be open to His voice and trust the direction in which He takes you. Find peace in the giving...and trust God for the rest.

PRAY: Dear Lord, please teach me to make You the center of my life in all things. Let me trust You to fulfill my needs in Your way, not through my own selfish will. To Your glory I offer all I have and all I am.

DAY Thirteen

**Waiting on God**

*I waited patiently for the Lord; He turned to me and heard my cry.*
*He lifted me out of the slimy pit, out of the mud and mire; He set my*
*feet on a rock and gave me a firm place to stand. He put a new song*
*in my mouth, a hymn of praise to our God.*
*(Psalm 40:1-3)*

It's been said that time heals all wounds. But when we're smack-dab in the middle of heartbreak it seems as if time is standing still. Life brings change and loss—it's inevitable. And, along with these changes, these losses, comes a measure of pain. It's tempting to numb the pain with worldly comforts such as drugs and alcohol. But God is the ultimate comforter. Cry to Him when your heart is wounded, and He will answer. He will dry your tears and turn your pain to joy. Trust in Him for all your needs.

Bow to God and cry out to Him. He knows your most intimate hurts...your deepest pain. Give everything to Him, and let Him carry the hurt for you. Seek His wisdom, and trust that He will answer you. In time, He will turn your pain to joy, and your tears to smiles.

REFLECT: God is the Master of the Universe. He formed you, and He knows you better than anyone here on earth could ever hope to. He has knocked at the door, and is patiently waiting for you to let Him in. He is the Great Healer, the Mighty Redeemer. Turn to Him and empty the hurt at His feet now—today.

PRAY: Dear Lord, when the winds howl and the waves

roll help me to turn toward You and seek Your guidance. Because I know that storms bring rainbows, and tears are followed by joy. You are the Giver of Life, My Rock and Fortress. In You alone will I trust.

DAY Fourteen

## Help Me, Dad

*This is what the Lord says, He who made the earth, the Lord who formed it and established it—the Lord is His name: "Call to Me and I will answer you and tell you great and unsearchable things you do not know."*
*(Jeremiah 33:2-3)*

Have you ever tried to teach a teenager, only to be demoted to the most lowly and unintelligent creature on earth? By their own account, teenagers know everything, and we—their parents—are simply clueless. Sometimes our own pride and selfish independence makes us teenagers in God's eyes. He wants us to listen, to learn, but we think He's clueless about what we really need. After all, we know best, right? In truth, it's only when we bow to God's will and we seek His guidance that we learn "great and unsearchable things."

The Lord formed the very earth where you live, and the ground upon which you travel in your daily walk. Surely, if you listen, you will find the treasure you've been seeking and learn the great things He is patiently waiting to tell you.

REFLECT: Relinquish your own selfish will and cry out to the Lord today. Consider all the times you've ignored His promptings or rejected His guidance. Ask Him to teach you His ways, and then listen for His answers.

PRAY: Lord, fill me with Your Holy Spirit and make me hungry for Your word. It's my fervent desire to grow closer to You and to gain spiritual maturity. Let my will bow to Yours as You reveal the awesome, boundless mystery of Your ways.

DAY Fifteen

**How May I Help You?**

*Serve Him with wholehearted devotion and with a willing mind, for the Lord searches every heart and understands every motive behind the thoughts. If you seek Him, He will be found by you.*
(*1 Chronicles 28:9*)

Walk into any restaurant and you are most likely greeted with, "How may I help you?" Bright smile...engaging eye contact...animated voice. This greeter has put his own needs aside and is completely focused on the task-at-hand. He's fresh-faced and eager to assist. He makes you feel glad to be there. This is the way God wants us to be when He walks through our door. He requests a willing heart and giving hands, a heart eager to do His work. And He knows the true purpose of those who come to serve.

Look around you for opportunities to serve Him today. Seek those in need and approach them with a smile and engaging eye contact. Welcome them warmly in His name and put your own needs and desires aside in order to serve. God welcomes a happy heart and giving hands—*your* heart and hands—as they cheerfully accomplish His work.

REFLECT: Consider ways you will be able to serve the Lord today. Can you offer a smile or a word of encouragement to someone in need? Grab every opportunity and watch the blessings flow. God has a servant's heart...strive to be more like Him.

PRAY: Lord, give me eyes like Yours to see where others may have a need that I can fill. Give me a smiling face and a willing heart and hands. Fill my mouth with encouraging words and my heart with the desire to serve.

DAY Sixteen

## The Man in the Mirror

*Do not listen to the word and so deceive yourselves. Do what it says.
Anyone who listens to the word but does not do what it says is like a
man who looks at his face in a mirror and, after looking at himself,
goes away and immediately forgets what he looks like.*
*(James 1:22-24)*

How many times have we asked our friends questions
such as, "Does this color look good on me?" or "Do these jeans
make me look fat?" We are oftentimes overly concerned about
our outward appearance while neglecting the inward
appearance of our heart and mind. Think about it. Have you
ever said to a friend, "Does this lie look bad on me?" or "Do
you think I hurt her by making that false promise?" What do
you think concerns God the most—the size of your jeans or the
size of your heart? The color of your shirt or the words that
flow from your lips?

Our Lord has set forth a guide book—the Bible—for our
thoughts, actions, and words. He didn't do this for himself—
He already knows what's desired and expected. Go into the
world as a person who remembers his place—as a child of
God. Cut the labels from your jeans and, instead, let the word
of God define you.

REFLECT: Have you read His word lately? Have you
soaked it in and taken it to heart? Begin today to draw closer
to God by setting aside time each day to study His word.
Make it a priority, as God has made you His priority.

PRAY: Lord, when the world bombards me with images of what it would have me be, help me to remember that my true beauty comes from serving You.

DAY Seventeen

## Are We There Yet?

*We pray this in order that you may live a life worthy of the Lord and
may please Him in every way: bearing fruit in every good work,
growing in the knowledge of God, being strengthened with all power
according to His glorious might so that you may have great
endurance and patience.*
*(Colossians 1:10-11)*

You know the drill…a small child rides in the backseat of
the car and his constant chatter is a distraction—and
sometimes an irritation—to the driver. Again, he asks, "Are
we there yet?" He wants the car to move faster, longs to arrive
at the destination. He is beyond impatient. In our daily walk
we are often like that child, scurrying at lightning speed from
one task to another, devoid of the simple pleasure of life's
journey and the landscape that forms our life. Time passes in a
blur, and when we do take a moment to grab a breath, we
wonder just how the hours turned into weeks, months, years.

Slow down. Enjoy the ride and drink in the scenery—a
sunrise, the laughter of a child, perhaps a friendly chat with a
neighbor. Discover the purpose of your actions and take few
minutes to thank God for the countless blessings in your life.
Soon, instead of the nagging, "Are we there yet?" you may
find yourself exclaiming, "Are we here *already*?"

REFLECT: Look around and discover the people you are
traveling through life with. What can you share with
them…including God's love?

PRAY: Lord, when life's hectic pace threatens to steal my

joy, let me remember the countless blessings You've bestowed upon me. Help me to appreciate Your boundless love that paints the world with children's laughter, kind words from a neighbor, and the beauty of a new sunrise.

DAY Eighteen

## Welcome Home

*Jesus said, "In my father's house are many rooms; if it were not so, I would have told you. I am going there to prepare a place for you. And if I go and prepare a place for you, I will come back and take you to be with me that you may also be where I am."*
*(John 14:2-3)*

When I was a little girl, about five years old, my large family went on a vacation to the Wisconsin Dells. Bundled in the backseat of our Chevy station wagon, we drove for what seemed like hours, and then spent a weekend in a hotel with an indoor swimming pool—a true adventure for me! When it was time to depart for home, my parents gathered all my siblings while I sat on the balcony overlooking the pool, captivated by shimmering, blue water. Soon, the lobby grew quiet; my parents had left—without me. Did I panic? No. I knew they would return for me as soon as they realized I was missing. They had promised, and I trusted their word. Soon, a boisterous commotion filled the lobby. My parents had returned, their arms outstretched to welcome me and tears streaming down their faces. I was precious in their sight.

Aren't we like that with God? He has promised to come back for us, and to take us to a place devoid of suffering and heartache. Do not panic...though we cannot see Him, He can see us. He knows our every thought and action, and He wants us to be with Him. One day He will return for us, arms outstretched and tears flowing down His face because we are with Him...and so very precious in His sight.

REFLECT: What are you doing while you wait for the return of our Lord and Savior? Do you spend time worrying about what will happen tomorrow? Don't worry. The Lord has promised us great things, and He will return. All things in this world pass away, but His love is forever. Fill your time with deeds that bring Him glory.

PRAY: Lord, when worry overwhelms help me to remember that You are in control. Pain and suffering will fade, replaced by the peace that only You can provide. Let me be joyful and diligent as I wait with hope for Your return.

DAY Nineteen

## Pulling the Wagon

*God gives strength to the weary and increases the power of the weak.*
*Even youths grow tired and weary and young men stumble and fall;*
*but those who hope in the Lord will renew their strength. They will*
*soar on wings like eagles; they will run and not grow weary; they*
*will walk and not faint.*
*(Isaiah 40:29-31)*

I am the second-eldest in a family of seven, and as a child I was often put in charge of my younger siblings. Sometimes, this responsibility included a trip to the store for milk or bread with my brother and sisters in tow, nestled together in a little red wagon. Of course, I was in charge of pulling the wagon—a load that seemed to weigh tons after walking a block or so in the blazing Chicago-summer sun. Sometimes I wanted to turn back home, to give up and admit to my parents that I was too weak to carry out the task. The walk, though only a few blocks, seemed like miles. But I knew they would be disappointed, so I continued on, putting one foot in front of the other along the concrete sidewalk while my younger siblings chattered merrily from behind.

Sometimes our walk with God seems insurmountable. The tasks we are asked to carry out are beyond our abilities, and the weight of responsibility weighs on us like tons of scrap metal. We want to give up. It's then that we must call on Him for help and guidance, and for the strength required to carry out what He wants us to do. With God's help, anything is possible.

REFLECT: Call on God today, and He will lighten your

load. He will walk beside you, pulling the wagon.

PRAY: Lord, when the burdens of life make me weary, help me to remember to call on You. Guide my feet so I do not stumble, and lift me up when I am weak. Make me strong as I run the race for You.

DAY Twenty

## The Chain of Life

*Make every effort to add to your faith goodness; and to goodness knowledge; and to knowledge self-control; and to self-control perseverance; and to perseverance godliness; and to godliness brotherly kindness; and to brotherly kindness, love. For if you possess these qualities in increasing measure, they will keep you from being ineffective and unproductive in your knowledge of our Lord Jesus Christ.*
*(2 Peter 1:6-8)*

Children love to make paper chains. It's a simple art project...requiring only scissors, paper, and a bit of glue. They work together, helping each other. One link nestles around another, and soon the chain grows long and strong. Faith is like this. A single link, such as goodness, leads to another...perhaps knowledge or self-control. We want to know more—to grow more—until the chain surrounds our life and spills into the lives of others. It's simple and requires only desire and the word of God as a guide for our lives. Together, we help each other form the chain and to carry out God's plan for our lives.

REFLECT: Today, take time to gather the tools to begin your own chain reaction. Stoke your desire to grow closer to God and to those around you. Take up your Bible and read. Ask Him to guide you as you begin your walk with Him. Soon, you'll begin to understand the way you should go— God's plan for you. Thus, the chain begins.

PRAY: Lord, today it is my desire to build a chain for You. Give me the tools of faith, goodness, knowledge, self-control, perseverance, brotherly kindness, and love. Help me to build the chain long and strong, so that I may be an example to others, and help draw them closer to You.

DAY Twenty-one

**God's Jewelry**

*A wife of noble character who can find? She is worth far more than
rubies...she is clothed with strength and dignity; she can laugh at
the days to come. She speaks with wisdom, and faithful instruction is
on her tongue.*
*(Proverbs 31:10, 25-26)*

My mom had a jewelry box on her dresser—a precious
gift from my dad on their wedding day. I'm sure he planned
to fill it with fine jewels—but God had other plans. Five
children later, the box wasn't much more than a play toy for
the kids. Mom never got the gold and diamonds she'd
dreamed of, but she didn't care. I doubt she ever missed the
man-made baubles. Instead, she wore God's jewelry—
boundless laughter, the ability to give heartfelt advice, the
strength and patience to dry our countless tears over the years.

What kind of jewelry do you wear? Is it the glitter of man-
made cubic zirconia, the cascade of diamond teardrops,
perhaps the splash of blood-red rubies? Or do you clothe
yourself in God's jewelry—the glow of patience, the shimmer
of kindness, and the vibrancy of wisdom?

REFLECT: Consider what you strive to adorn yourself
with. Talk to God today. Ask Him to dress you in His jewels—
strength, dignity, laughter, and wisdom.


PRAY: Lord, though the media would have me believe
otherwise, I know that true beauty comes only from the
garments You provide: strength, dignity, wisdom, laughter,

and faith that grows through Your instruction. Fill me with the desire to grow closer to You. Help me not to want the passing glitter of this world, and adorn me with Your priceless jewelry.

DAY Twenty-two

## What's in Your Toolbox?

*Each one should use whatever gift he has received to serve others,
faithfully administering God's grace in its various forms. If anyone
speaks, he should do it as one speaking the very words of God. If
anyone serves, he should do it with the strength God provides, so
that in all things God may be praised through Jesus Christ.*
*(1 Peter 4:10-11)*

My dad was a builder. He had the gift to take a few two-by-fours and a handful of nails and create beautiful and sturdy structures. In his toolbox, he carried all he needed—hammer, tape-measure, screwdrivers in various sizes. I loved to delve inside the box, to examine and handle each item. Their power—the fact that these tools could work together to create amazing things—captivated me. My dad was strong; he could do anything and everything with his tools.

Each of us is like my dad. We all have our own set of tools, compliments of God. Perhaps you are blessed with hospitality, or a deep sense of compassion, or the ability to speak in front of large crowds. Maybe you sing like an angel, or have the ability to organize charity events. Or maybe, like my dad, you have the gift to take a piece of lumber and fashion it into a room—or a building. It's our responsibility—and our calling—to seek God's wisdom concerning what's in our own personal toolbox.

REFLECT: Ask God today to help you examine the gifts in *your* toolbox so you can take each out, dust each off, and begin to serve Him.

PRAY: Lord, please unveil my tools and give me a willing and eager heart to use them for Your good. Thank you for making me unique in the gifts I bring to Your kingdom. Let me never take them for granted, and, should I ever grow weary of the work, help me to remember just how precious each job is.

DAY Twenty-three

**God Stands Guard**

*Do not be anxious about anything, but in everything, by prayer and petition, with thanksgiving, present your requests to God. And the peace of God, which transcends all understanding, will guard your hearts and your minds in Jesus Christ.*
(Philippians 4:6-7)

To most of us, our homes are precious possessions... places where we gather with family and friends in fellowship. From time to time, news of a home invasion sparks fear at our very core. We worry that our house, too, will be assaulted if we are not vigilant in protecting the premise. So, perhaps, we install a security system. Well, with God there's no need to have fear for anything. He is the security system for our lives. With God, no real harm can touch us. His gift to us is peace, even in the midst of trial, hardship—and home invasion—if we ask for and accept it. God is the Almighty Protector.

When you feel afraid, cry out to Him and be reassured. Soon, fear and worry will be replaced by trust. God is the Master of the Universe...your own personal security system. He cares for you, and wants you to seek His protection in all things. So, turn to Him today, and find peace.

REFLECT: Immerse yourself in God's word. Read His passages of promise and protection and be assured His words are His own personal gift for *you*.

PRAY: Lord, when I feel vulnerable, let me remember that you are the Almighty Protector. Each day, I will clothe myself in Your armor and ask for Your gift of peace.

DAY Twenty-four

## Black Friday

*I will lead the blind by the ways they have not known, along unfamiliar paths I will guide them; I will turn the darkness into light before them and make the rough places smooth. These are the things I will do; I will not forsake them.*
*(Isaiah 42:16)*

The Friday after Thanksgiving is the frenzied shopping day traditionally known as Black Friday. Hordes of people across the country rise well before daybreak to claim their places in the most sought-after shopping lines. And they wait…and wait to purchase bargains. As I consider this, I wonder…what is so black about the beginning of the holiday season—the season of our Savior's birth? Shouldn't the day be called "Bright Friday" or "The Friday of Light"? When God sent His Son to earth the darkness became light and hope replaced fear. What an amazing event! And, better yet, the light of Jesus shines way beyond the hours of a single day—it shines for all eternity.

Do you approach God with the same enthusiasm that shoppers approach their bargain trip? As many seek the best deal, do you seek His light as the greatest bargain?

REFLECT: Consider how many times you rush toward something important. Today, rush from the darkness, from the incompleteness in the world, and toward the light. Follow the path God has set before you. Ask Him to guide your every step. He is waiting for you with His promise to make your paths smooth and to fill you with hope for the future.

PRAY: Dear Lord, today and every day, I seek Your light in a world that is often filled with darkness. Place before me a path and guide my every step so I may always walk full of hope and in Your light.

DAY Twenty-five

## The Anchor

*An anxious heart weighs a man down, but a kind word cheers him up.*
*(Proverbs 12:25)*

The water cooler at work is a popular place where we can catch up on the latest news—and the latest gossip. Sometimes we worry...is a coworker more popular? Did someone else get that promotion we were vying for? Or, perhaps, we witnessed co-workers in some activity outside work that appeared to be less-than-honorable, and we're just checking our facts with others. Harsh words and gossip are like an anchor to the soul. When we focus on the negative, we are weighed down as if an anchor is attached to our hearts...dragging others into the depths along with us.

Do you lift up others, or do your words drag them to the depths of despair? Is the water cooler a place to share God's love or a place to fill with darkness? From this day forward, make an active effort to spread kindness and good cheer. Turn your anchor into a life raft...one word at a time.

REFLECT: Take a personal inventory. Be cognizant of the words that flow from your mouth. How many are negative? How many positive?

PRAY: Let the words from my mouth be only positive. It's my desire, Lord, to toss my anchor aside and instead build a life raft to rescue others from the depths of darkness and despair. Use me, Lord, to share with others the love, peace, and grace that only You can provide.

DAY Twenty-six

## Cruise Control

*When you pass through the waters, I will be with you; and when you pass through the rivers, they will not sweep over you. When you walk through the fire, you will not be burned; the flames will not set you ablaze.*
(Isaiah 43:2)

My dad was a good man—eager to serve those in need and always ready to offer advice or encouragement. He did not draw attention to himself, and often helped others anonymously. But he had one quirk that drove me crazy as a teenager with a driver's license. Whenever we traveled, he demanded to be seated behind the wheel. Dad had to be in control, driving himself to all destinations. He could not bring himself to trust others to get him there safely.

As he aged, he was no longer able to drive and had to relent...to give up control. Amazingly enough, he enjoyed the freedom to take in the scenery and to share in conversation without focusing on potholes and detours along the road.

Aren't we like my dad when it comes to trusting God to get us where we need to go? We want to keep our hands on the wheel...just in case. After all, we know the way better than He does, right? Relinquishing control is one of the hardest things—and one of the greatest roadblocks—for us.

REFLECT: Consider how often you try to take control of a situation instead of surrendering to God completely and trusting Him to work in your life. Let go of the wheel and let God take the driver's seat. He knows the path that is meant for you. Trust Him to take you there, and enjoy the scenery along the way.

PRAY: Lord, remove my stubborn will and teach me to relinquish the wheel to You. Let me not block the blessings You have planned for me with my selfish need to be in control. I trust in You for all my needs and protection. For You alone, Lord, know the plans You have for me.

DAY Twenty-seven

## Do You See What I See?

*No one lights a lamp and puts it in a place where it will be hidden, or under a bowl. Instead, he puts it on its stand, so that those who come in may see the light. Your eye is the lamp of your body. When your eyes are good, your whole body also is full of light. But when they are bad, your body is also full of darkness. See to it, then, that the light within you is not darkness.*
*(Luke 11:33-35)*

Our society is bombarded with billboards and commercials that gratify sex, immorality, and worldly possessions. We're immersed in the hype, and it's impossible to avoid the message unless we become recluses, shutting ourselves away from the world. As Christians, we are called to guard our eyes and our hearts, yet we must live in a world that condones immorality and selfishness. How do we manage to find a balance and keep our hearts and minds pure and filled with God's light?

Think of yourself as a beacon…a lighthouse amid dark and stormy waters. Use your light to lead others to safe shores. When beams are gathered together, the light is more powerful, so gather others close in fellowship with other faithful Christians. Together, fuel your light with God's word, holding it strong and steady. Wherever you find darkness, share your light.

REFLECT: Consider ways in which you might separate yourself from the immorality in the world. Perhaps it's by not watching a particular television show, or by not frequenting a certain hang-out, and instead using that time to fellowship with others who are striving to be *in* the world but not *of* the world. Call on God to help you, and He will strengthen you. Ask Him to make you courageous in sharing your love for Him.

PRAY: Lord, it's my desire to turn away from the darkness of this world. Fill my eyes with the light of Your word. Give me the courage to share Your word with others. Let me stand tall, and remove all fear from me. I long to be a beacon, drawing others to You.

DAY Twenty-eight

**Waiting for the Honey**

*The testing of your faith develops perseverance. Perseverance must finish its work so that you may be mature and complete, not lacking anything.*
*(James 1:3-4)*

I have a friend who makes honey—she keeps bees and distributes their honey in quart-sized jars to friends. When she delivers a jar, the instructions are simple…the honey won't go bad unless you dip a sugar-laden spoon into it, thus breaking it down and compromising the freshness. Not too difficult, right? Except when the honey gets to the bottom of the jar, and the only spoon you have is laced with sugar. You upturn the jar and wiggle. And wait…and wait for the sweet brown texture to flow into your coffee-cup. But honey is stubborn, and soon you find yourself dipping that sugary spoon—despite the warning. The honey is ruined.

Life is like that. Sometimes we become so impatient to have what we desire that we do exactly what we know we shouldn't, despite the inevitable negative outcome. As God watches, I imagine He weeps for our impulsiveness and poor choices, the result of free will.

REFLECT: Consider times you've acted out of impatience and resolve in future to step back and breathe before acting. Read God's word and develop patience. Trust that all things happen for our good with God's timing—not our timing. Learn to wait for the honey.

PRAY: Lord, instill in me patience that allows me to wait

for the sweetness that is Your perfect honey. I bow to You, and relinquish my will to Yours. It's my fervent desire to develop maturity and perseverance so that I may trust in You alone. Create a work in me, Lord, that draws me closer to You.

DAY Twenty-nine

## Childhood Wishes

*Jesus Christ is the same yesterday and today and forever.*
*(Hebrews 13:8)*

Childhood is a magical time...a time of dreams, wishes and hopes. This is especially true during the Christmas season. I remember fondly the days of my childhood, when I watched the mail for the annual Sears catalogue. Each holiday season, it arrived in colorful glory, full of treasures I hoped to receive. I'd haul the oversized magazine to the living room couch and snuggle along with my siblings, each of us marking our favorite items...our Christmas wishes. Each year the selection changed—new toys, more fashionable styles. Out with the old, in with the new.

Unlike the catalogue of my childhood, God's word—the Bible—does not change. It doesn't fade as clothing tends to do when washed. It doesn't wear out, no matter how much it's studied and used. The message never goes out of fashion. The words are the same as yesterday, and will remain today, tomorrow, and through the years to come. The message will sustain you all your days...not just during the Christmas season.

REFLECT: Study the Bible as you studied the Christmas catalogue of your childhood. God's word is filled with hope...a message that remains strong and true. Become familiar with the passages, and tuck them deep within your heart.

PRAY: Lord, I wait for You with the eager hope of a child

on Christmas Eve. Fill my heart with Your message and sustain me with the knowledge that You are the same today, tomorrow, and always.

DAY Thirty

**Seasons**

*There is a time for everything, and a season for every activity under heaven: a time to be born and a time to die, a time to plant and a time to uproot, a time to kill and a time to heal, a time to tear down and a time to build, a time to weep and a time to laugh, a time to mourn and a time to dance, a time to scatter stones and a time to gather them, a time to embrace and a time to refrain, a time to search and a time to give up, a time to keep and a time to throw away, a time to tear and a time to mend, a time to be silent and a time to speak, a time to love and a time to hate, a time for war and a time for peace.*
*(Ecclesiastes 3:1-8)*

My grandfather loved the change of seasons. He'd sit in his backyard and sniff the fresh air, sighing, "'bout time for the season to change. I wonder what's in store." While others bemoaned the simmering heat of summer or the blustery chill of winter, my grandfather welcomed each new day—each season—with delight. He knew the purpose in each shift of the weather...to provide for reflection on days passed and for the anticipation of days to come.

As in nature, God provides seasons for our spiritual lives. We laugh, we cry, we make new friends and lose others. Sometimes we want to leap for joy, and other times scream with frustration.

REFLECT: What season are you in, and how do you lean on God for guidance through this season and into the next? Take a moment to reflect and anticipate...it's what God desires from you.

PRAY: Lord, help me to trust in You through every season of my life...laughter and tears, poverty and wealth. You are the Master of the Universe and the Giver of Life. I place my hope in You for all eternity.

DAY Thirty-one

## The Tree of Life

*"'Blessed is the man who trusts in the Lord, whose confidence is in Him. He will be like a tree planted by the water, that sends out its roots by the stream. It does not fear when heat comes; its leaves are always green. It has no worries in a year of drought and never fails to bear fruit.'"*
*(Jeremiah 17:7-8)*

My grandparents were both expert gardeners. They studied and experimented with different types of seeds and learned by trial and error over the course of many years. On one side of the yard, my grandmother grew an explosion of beautiful, fragrant flowers, while on the other side my grandfather cultivated a myriad of delicious vegetables. But, no matter the strength of their green thumbs, when the Chicago winters blew in, the plants inevitably died or, in some cases, went dormant until the following spring.

God's love for us never grows dormant. He is here for us whatever the weather. He desires for us to develop a green thumb for Him—to cultivate our faith and grow the fruits of His Spirit through the study of His word, the Bible. We don't have to learn by trial and error, like my grandparents did. We can nurture a garden of wisdom through His word.

REFLECT: Have you cultivated a knowledge of God's word and will? Pick up your Bible today and dust it off and study God's message. Plant His words into the soil of your heart and soon your own garden of wisdom will begin to flourish.

PRAY: Lord, I know Your love for me is ever-present and never grows dormant. I desire to seek a closer relationship with You. Develop in me the good habit of studying Your message. Cultivate the fruits of Your Spirit in me.

*My Personal Wisdom Tree Notes*

_____

_____

_____

_____

_____

_____

_____

_____

_____

_____

_____

_____

_____

_____

_____

_____

_____

_____

_____

_____

_____

_____

_____

_____

Thank you for purchasing this White Rose Publishing title. For other inspirational stories, please visit our on-line bookstore at www.pelicanbookgroup.com.

For questions or more information, contact us at titleadmin@pelicanbookgroup.com.

White Rose Publishing
*Where Faith is the Cornerstone of Love*™
an imprint of Pelican Ventures Book Group
www.PelicanBookGroup.com

May God's glory shine through
this inspirational work of fiction.

AMDG